MY TEARS OF TOMORROW

Bound by Love, Defined by Loss

based on a true story

E.H. KIM

HYO Publishing

DEDICATION

Kalebee - my son and my life, you don't have to hide your tears or hide the pain from me – I understand. You are the reason I keep going and the reason I smile. Your eyes are sad but know that my pain will always be bearable as long as you try to smile. This life is one fun ride with you, and I am one lucky mommy to have you as my son. No one knows what level I'm going to end this game at, but I finally finished this for you. You always make me proud…the wind.

TABLE OF CONTENTS

CHAPTER ONE
Shattered Equilibrium

...one...two...three... the tears keep falling down my face.

Wiping them away with my sleeve feels futile, as their flow seems unending. Life has trapped hope in suspended animation, leaving death as the only conceivable outcome. Hope is frozen in abeyance, leaving me to drown in desperation. A glimmer of light lingers at the edge of my vision. I focus on it, desperately trying to hold onto it and breathe some substance into it before the darkness overwhelms me once again and hope is lost forever. With every breath and ray of light pouring down into my soul, I know this may be my last chance to find hope. And so I cling to that thin thread of possibility with all my will.

When will the shadows stop tormenting me? The sorrowful recollections in my mind remain, and my tears fail to wash them away. These memories are becoming too heavy for me to bear.

Mondays, those seemingly ordinary days that cyclically mark the beginning of a new week, take on a profoundly ominous air as this particular Monday unveils itself. It heralds the dawning of an arduous journey, fraught with unrelenting pain that lay strewn across the path I was fated to take. I stand at the edge of a precipitous cliff, my world crumbling beneath me like a house of cards, threatening to cast me into the abyss below. Every ounce of my being aches from the unbearable weight of my existence and I find myself barely clinging on, desperate for something to keep me anchored in place. Despite all the turmoil, a part of me yearns to forget and give in to the call of gravity, allowing myself to fall into nothingness and free myself from this agonizing torment.

I can almost make out his silent words, comforting me, telling me that everything will be okay. But shattered is my once-familiar routine, and what was once a normal life has become an unfamiliar landscape. Time assumes a paradoxical state, simultaneously frozen and rushing forward at an uncontrollable speed, leaving me with a sense of impending doom as time is running out. Amidst this disarray, silence reigns, accompanied by an emptiness that feels profound beyond words.

With a knot of dread clenched in my chest, I step forward onto this ominous road, fully aware of the unspeakable challenges and heartache that is lurking at each turn. Every moment becomes a fight against my own inner turmoil, as I strive to retain a semblance of sanity. My despair is slowly trying to tear me apart piece by piece. Through all the darkness and despair, traces of faint light shine through, reminding me that even in these moments of terror, there is still something worth fighting for.

The walls are sterile white, and the chairs are cold and worn, chipped and cracked. They have the texture of soft, dried leather, worn and polished smooth by endless sittings. The edges are marked by years of countless hands grasping and pulling on the splintering wood. Seated in the somber waiting room, an oppressive silence surrounds me, amplifying the weight of my prayers as they reverberate through the corridors of my mind. Profound uncertainty tightens its grip on my heart, each passing moment intensifying the torment. Clinging desperately to a flicker of hope, I pray that the outcome awaiting me is not dire. Beside me, my mother and brother sit in silence, our hands intertwined in a display of shared vulnerability and fear. As we occupy the chairs aligned against the wall, a tangible mix of anticipation and dread engulfs us, as if we are engaged in a fierce struggle against the specter of devastating news. Together, we yearn for the best possible outcome amidst the haunting presence of the worst.

Caught in the crossfire of conflicting thoughts, my mind became a battleground, where each negative notion faced a relentless opponent, fighting to dismiss them as insignificant. This psychological turmoil wages war within me, leaving me caught in the crossfire of absolute doubt and uncertainty. As the sliding door opens, offering a glimpse into the examination room, a familiar dread washes over me, causing my heart to plummet. With each passing nurse and doctor, my heart hesitantly begins its ascent, seeking its rightful place within me, hoping to settle without causing further anguish. Time dragged on mercilessly requiring ultimate patience and trust in the total strangers who would be the only ones able to bring comfort to my family in this given moment. With each passing minute, the anticipation builds in weight until it becomes unbearable.

I know our turn had come as the exam room door suddenly slams open again. Striding into the room with purpose, a disquieting shadow spread like fog from its body over the floor. Her white coat hung to her knees, and her stethoscope draped around her neck, she strode purposefully toward us, her cold eyes betraying no emotion. A wave of dread washes over me, as I brace myself for whatever news is about to come. Is this the mix of hope and fear that others experience in moments like these? Tears swell within me as I anticipate the flood of turbulent emotions about to consume my being. It seems I am destined to dwell in a realm shrouded in tears with an overflow of emotions that I have yet to learn to control.

In that pivotal moment, my mind reels, and I feel as though my heart will burst. All time seems to have stopped as I stand in the doorway, sensing an impending doom from the doctor who has been entrusted with deciding my dad's fate. My heart races, grappling with the incomprehensible ability of its uncanny capacity to discern that this doctor emerging from the door holds within her the power to end life as I know it. She tells us that he is ready to see us and that we can all proceed to the exam room and nods in the direction of the sliding doors.

Taking a trembling step into the room, the anticipation of the unseen danger only increases with each passing second. The choking silence threatens to drown me in a swirling vortex of fear and anxiety. Nothing is revealed about the nature of the news that awaits me. Even a subtle hint would have been welcome, but heavy silence hangs in the air along with an endless sea of unanswered questions. My eyes lock onto his black socks peeking out from beneath the sheets, and they are a stark reminder of his mortality. Amidst the hushed whispers, only one voice pierces through—his poignant inquiry, 'Where is my daughter?' The weight of those words bears down on my heart like a train barreling down at full speed. As I inch forward, it is as if every step summons forth a stronger force of gravity upon me—a warning sign that his life could be lost forever. I am completely unprepared to face the unknown and terrified of what tomorrow will bring.

I attempt to force my mind to crawl away from the thoughts of death, determined to suspend reality as long as possible. I desperately cling to the edges of my sanity that I know I'm losing, praying that this will somehow change the outcome. I stand outside the door, my trembling hands pressed against the cold metal frame. I could feel the tears running down my face like a waterfall, cold and sharp against my skin. My chin trembled as I tried to stifle a sob rising from within my chest. Each drop is like an icy needle, charged with regret and sadness that burns my cheeks with its intensity.

Desperate to keep the emotions inside, I force a weak smile to my lips - barely managing to mask the pain brewing in me. With trembling hands, I quickly wipe away the tears with my sleeve, hoping that nothing would give away the storm of feelings raging inside me. With a shaky breath, I force a faint smile onto my lips – hoping it is enough to mask the avalanche of emotions that I'm feeling. I took a deep breath and uttered those three words as if they were infused with both determination and fear: "Here I am!"

The man, who had been accustomed to wearing suits, now lay on the hard and uncomfortable hospital bed, clad in a measly worn-out hospital gown. His features were illuminated with a gentle smile as he whispered to me, "I'm ok.." In his assurance that everything would be alright, a glimmer of hope began to take root. How could he possibly possess such certainty? I want to believe him, but I am scared; scared to let the lies take root in my mind and give me false hope no matter how much I need to hear it.

At this moment, all I crave is something… anything… anyone… lighten my burden and help me through whatever lies ahead. With a brave yet fragile smile, I hold my breath, praying that the tears teetering on the precipice of my eyes will dissipate alongside the pain that threatens to consume me at any given moment. In the realm of his reassurance, as long as he says that he is ok, it will suffice, even if it is just momentarily. I resolve to persistently affirm to myself that he will overcome this ordeal. Now, let us see where this uncertain path will lead us, and maybe fate will spare me from being the sole straggler left behind.

In that dreaded moment, the bitterest of words pierced my ears and tore away the last shred of hope to which I clung: "Your dad has advanced Stage IV gastric cancer."

CHAPTER TWO
Dark Reality

The doctor's words crash against me like a tidal wave, drowning my senses and submerging my mind in a sea of abject terror. His diagnosis of advanced Stage IV gastric cancer cuts through the air like a blade, tearing apart the fragile equilibrium of my existence. The air grows thick around me, each breath becomes a struggle against an invisible weight pressing against my chest. My throat tightens, constricting like a vice, and even the smallest inhale feels like trying to draw in air through a narrow straw. Every lungful is a battle, each exhale is a release of pent-up tension. It is as if the very atmosphere has turned against me, squeezing the life out of me with each passing moment. Everything around me slows down, each second crystallizing until I feel suspended in time, struggling to comprehend the gravity of losing him forever. A thousand questions loop endlessly within my head, but no answers seem to surface, only despair and emptiness.

"Don't cry, I will be okay," he whispers to me.

But how can everything be okay? His words trigger a tidal wave of grief that crashes against my chest. He takes my hand in his, and I can feel the roughness of his skin - a texture that was crafted over time like a mountain created through many cycles. The grip he has on me is tight, almost as if conveying a silent message of strength and hope. He radiates warmth like the sun, and melts away the chill from my frozen hands, momentarily mending the broken pieces inside me. The words "gastric cancer" reverberates within me like a funeral dirge, reminding me that our lives have been irrevocably changed, and there is no turning back.

At that moment, the doctor's voice fades into an endless background, her words becoming nothing more than scattered noise. How could this be our reality? It feels like the ground beneath me is crumbling, leaving me in a state of profound disbelief. The weight of the diagnosis presses upon me, suffocating any semblance of hope. This very moment is when I realize that my life has become exhausting and terrifying in one blow with absolute fear of losing someone whom I love the most in this world. This is one deepening sadness, and my tears just keep falling. There's not much time left.

Questions flood my mind, each one more haunting than the previous. How could this be happening? What would life be like without my dad? I am afraid to entertain these thoughts, fearing that by doing so, I will somehow manifest them into existence. He had always been strong and seemingly healthy, but now I realize that this insidious disease has been silently wreaking havoc inside him, unbeknownst to us. Could there have been a mistake? Amid this storm of emotions, I cling to the desperate hope that this is all a misdiagnosis, a cruel twist of fate.

The room was silent, save for the faint ticking of the clock on the wall. I stare out the window, lost in my thoughts. Overwhelmed by a sense of dread, an intangible fear wraps around me like a dense fog. The uncertainty clouding my thoughts and casting a dark shadow over our once-happy lives. How could I face the prospect of a future without my dad? The world seemed like a bleak and unfamiliar place, devoid of the warmth and security that only he provides. I desperately longed for this nightmare to be just that—a figment of my imagination, a cruel trick played by fate.

But I knew in my heart that it wasn't, and I found myself grateful, in some strange way, for the few moments of peace I had left. I close my eyes and take a deep breath, determined to cling to the present and whatever joys it still has left in store. Time was running out faster than imaginable and I wanted to savor every moment I have with him.

I am aware that pretending it's not happening will not spare us from the reality of our situation. The path ahead of us will be hard and filled with incredible struggles. We need to find every bit of strength and resilience we have to conquer the unexplored realm of cancer. However, amidst all these shadows, a glimmer of hope lingers on, encouraging us to hang on and trust in the possibility of being healed, of miracles.

As tears well in my eyes and begin to spill over, I fight to remain strong for my dad. I can't let him see the depths of my anguish, the overwhelming fear that consumes me. I need to be his rock, his source of unwavering support. But deep inside, I grapple with the devastating reality of the diagnosis, struggling to reconcile the vibrant, loving dad before me with the harsh truth of his illness. We embark on this daunting journey, I know that we have to face the truth head-on, with courage and determination. Both of which I lack. This seems like a losing battle on my part. Gastric cancer has forever altered the landscape of our lives, and our only choice is to confront it.

In the blink of an eye, my world is shattered into a million pieces. How can everything crumble so swiftly, leaving me bewildered and absolutely lost? A torrent of questions floods my mind, but answers remain elusive, leaving me stranded in a sea of uncertainty. The deafening silence that follows emphasizes the magnitude of the situation, amplifying my anxiety and fear.

Among the myriad of questions that haunt me, one looms ominously above all others: How much time does he have left? It is a question I hesitate to even contemplate, for its weight is unbearable. An answer I am not ready to accept. Time, once an abstract concept, suddenly became a precious commodity slipping through my fingers like grains of sand. The whirlwind of emotions is so overwhelming, I watch my mother assist my dad in getting dressed as we are told that we can leave. Left in a state of limbo, our next step was to await a call to learn about our options once the biopsy results from this visit are reviewed.

Hanging on the wall across the hospital exam bed are two large TVs used as monitors – one showed the MRI that was done that reflected all the cancer spots by lighting up in white every place there was a tumor and another one that was a snapshot in color that reflects the scan that was done of my dad's stomach. I couldn't help but think of it as a horrible bag of popcorn that had been spilled and draped in a dark red blanket of blood, evidence of an insidious intruder invading my dad's body. The image will forever be burned into my mind as a horrifying revelation - a visual manifestation of the cancer's devastating presence.

Cancer, often referred to as a "silent killer," has silently woven its way through my dad's stomach, completely undetectable until it has advanced to an alarming stage. The grim reality becomes clear—the cancer has progressed too far for a simple removal of his stomach, and his age poses challenges for radiation treatment. The road ahead looms menacingly, the darkness of its uncertain path swallowing us whole. My breath catches in my throat as I see the unyielding cage of suffering that this disease has created, without hope and with no way out. The initial shock has settled into a cold and harsh reality, forcing me to confront the harsh truths we face and the urgency of time that he does not have slipping away.

Numbness engulfs my being as I make my way out of the exam room, the weight of despair tugging at my heart. It feels as if my heart has somehow managed to detach itself, falling into an abyss of sorrow, its heaviness unbearable. Just when I thought it could not hurt anymore. The hospital floors, adorned with white spotted tiles, stretched out before me like an endless pathway leading to inevitable loss and grief. Each step I take feels laborious, like it will be the last one I ever take on this earth. Cancer – this one word had the power to push me further into a world of darkness.

Navigating the hallways, my mind struggles to comprehend the events that just unfolded. A part of me clings desperately to the hope that it was all a mistake, an erroneous diagnosis that can be rectified. Maybe we need another opinion? A second? Third? Deep down, I know that my silent pleas will not alter the reality before me. This painful truth becomes my new reality, one that I must face. The weight of grief intensifies, threatening to shatter the fragile composure I have mustered. Yet, somehow, I summon the strength to keep moving forward, driven by an indomitable will to shield my dad from the sadness that is drowning me. I am determined to hide my pain, to present a facade of strength, even as I crumble inside.

As I turn to glance back, I see that my mother and brother remain in the room, their presence a temporary shield that allows me a moment of respite. I find solace in the silent tears that stream down my face, blurring my vision. All around me, the world is fading to gray, and I feel like my heart is being ripped to shreds with each passing second.

In this private moment of anguish, the weight of the word "death" echoes through my mind, reminding me of the imminent loss of someone I hold dearer than life itself. My throat constricts as I try to swallow back the sobs that threaten to escape me, and I can only stand there in a daze, unable to comprehend the tragedy that has befallen us. I can feel the finality of the situation. I looked around as if everything had become a blur with my tears masking my eyes. I knew that nothing would ever be the same again.

… I can't do this. No matter how hard I try, I can't do this. Please make me numb. God, take this pain away. How can I become strong enough to handle this? Silence. The answer lingers in deathly silence, mocking me with its emptiness.

My hands tremble as I enter the elevator, and my facade of control crumbles. Tears stream uncontrollably down my face, defying all my attempts to hide them. Unable to hold back the flood of tears any longer, I concede to the overwhelming grief that consumes me. The facade I so desperately clung to crumbles, revealing the raw vulnerability that lies beneath. The realization that I cannot bear this burden alone, that I cannot face the impending loss without crumbling becomes painfully clear.

As the elevator doors close and as it makes its descent to the first floor, I collapse against the wall, surrendering to the overwhelming wave of emotions that consume me. The buttons blur before my tear-filled eyes, but I manage to find and press "1." At least my dad was not able to see me fall apart. The elevator's buttons are blurs of red, white, and black. The LED screen, advertising an upcoming exhibit, is flashing bright white. The foreign pattern stabs at the back of my eyes. The hum of machinery, carrying the elevator to the third floor, is a low drone like an idling engine. Descending from the third floor of the hospital feels like an escape, a desperate attempt to distance myself from the reality that has just shattered my world.

The wall of emotions I had built to keep my pain at bay caved in and fell apart. Tears flooded my eyes, and I pressed my hand over my mouth in fear that sobs would escape. The moment I let the wall crumble, it felt like a thunderstorm echoing in my chest. My heart throbbed with immeasurable sadness and grief, and sorrow raged through me. It was overwhelming indeed—the wrenching pain of having your heart ripped from you and destroyed before you could fix it. I allow myself to feel it all—the unbearable pain of loss and the heartbreaking realization that no one will ever be there for me the way he had always been. Even though I had just heard the news with my mom and my brother a few minutes ago, the feeling of being alone was terrifying. It was an overwhelming onslaught, but I found that instead of fighting it off, I could surrender to the torrent of feelings and embrace the depth of my pain.

The tears came faster than I could have ever imagined. I felt the burning sensation of saltwater rushing past my cheeks, running down into the depths of my soul. My memories and dreams, my hopes and desires were spilling out from behind my eyes. The pain remains, but a heavy burden was pressing down on my shoulders. I realize that I have no option but to let go of what once was and embrace the new reality even if it hurts me to do so. My soul aches, yet I have no choice but to keep going forward, no matter how uncomfortable or bittersweet the journey may be. I don't want to lose him.

Each floor passes like an eternity, as I struggle to find some semblance of strength within myself. Memories of my dad flood my mind, each one a reminder of the love we shared and the impending loss that looms before me. The pain feels insurmountable, and I wonder how I will ever find the courage to face the days to come without him. The solitude of the empty elevator offers a brief respite, a sanctuary where I can freely cry. I wish for something to happen, no matter how disastrous, anything that will free me from reality, be it the elevator plummeting or the doors opening to become a portal.

The elevator reaches the ground floor, and the doors open with a soft chime. The world outside continues, unaware of the pain and sadness I felt inside. Nothing outside changed, yet everything appears so different. I gather up what little strength I have inside me and take one step at a time. Wandering through the lobby, I feel lost and broken like a ship in a violent storm. I quickly made my way towards to the exit, eager to leave the place that was now filled with such dreadful reminders of what was to come. As I walked out the revolving doors, a gust of cold air rushed over me, sending a shiver down my spine. I instinctively turned my head back for one last look at the hospital, a place that had once provided solace, but now felt completely devoid of comfort. Taking a deep breath, I step out into the world unprepared to face whatever comes next.

I trudge slowly from the hospital entrance, my feet dragging with every step, and my gaze is transfixed on the asphalt. The chill in the air feels like a blanket of sadness draped around me. The car looks so far away and seems to be looming closer as I move further away. When I finally reach it, I pause for a moment and wipe away tears streaming down my face. My hands shake uncontrollably as I insert the key and bring the engine to life. I shift into gear, releasing a sob into the quietness before heading out onto the road. Time passes by excruciatingly slowly - it feels like an eternity - as each streetlight shines brighter than the last. The drive home feels like an eternity, my thoughts running wild, and my heart broken.

The tears were replaced by a numbness that settled within me. My emotions drained and replaced by an emptiness that eerily matched the hollow ache in my heart. It felt like there was nothing left inside me but a cavernous shell where my soul used to reside. I am consumed by thoughts of confusion, doubt, and disbelief. What do I have to do? What is it all for? The questions keep circling in my head. A growing sense of dread seeps into the corners of my mind and settles there like an unwelcome visitor with no intention of leaving.

I drive on, my destination known but my mind unclear. As I enter the familiar streets of my neighborhood, I feel like a stranger in a foreign land. Nothing was the same, and nothing would ever be again. I take the long way home, driving in circles so that I can cry what remaining tears I seem to have, desperate to put off the inevitability of returning home. The sadness that had taken over my body was absolutely unbearable, and so deep that I don't recognize myself. I had never felt such sadness before, yet here it was, consuming me completely.

I pulled my car to the side of the road and stare at the old red brick house. My parents and brother had yet to arrive, which meant that I had some time left to recoup myself. My hands grip the steering wheel tightly, envisioning crashing it into the concrete wall ahead. My chin quivers as tears sting my cheeks once again. If only I could go back in time, go back to being a little girl again with no worries, and just play in the yard with my dad. The shadows of my past dance around the lawn. I want to run away, to disappear, to forget this has ever happened, but I know that would only make things worse. I have to be strong for them, even though I feel like I am barely hanging on by a thread. I wipe away my tears with the sleeve of my shirt, staining the fabric as I attempt to compose myself before my family arrives. I don't want my dad to see how much I've cried or the fact that I did cry, fearing that it will only add to his sadness. I've been reduced to a withered shell of flesh and bone filled with brokenness and emptiness. Taking a deep breath, I attempt to cover up the tears with the little foundation compact. The jagged pieces of my broken heart are temporarily masked by plastering a thin smile across my face, a facade that will shield them from all my emotions.

The crunch of the gravel beneath our feet was the only sound that filled the air as I stepped out of the car. I immediately noticed the sense of dread that hung in the atmosphere like a thick fog. My mother seemed to shrink in on herself, her face turning a ghostly white as she took a deep breath and slowly walked toward the house with my dad. My brother trails behind, his head down, and his hands nervously fidgeting.

I follow my family up the driveway, every step feeling like it was leading me closer and closer to the unknown. I could feel my heart pounding in my chest, the anticipation of what I was about to encounter making my palms sweaty and my stomach churn. I pause for a moment at the entrance of the house, gathering my courage before I open the door to step inside.

The house was just as we had left it—empty. The furniture that once held moments of joy and laughter now stood in overbearing silence. I look around, remembering the days we had spent here together, and the pain of losing my dad was unbearable. I move past my mother and brother, suddenly embracing my dad with everything I have left. Spoken words of love and hope pour out of me like an incantation, an impassioned plea for him to pull through this darkness, even though deep down, I know they are mere words. Lies that I desperately hope to be true.

My silent plea hangs in the air between us - one he can't answer - and yet it feels like his embrace gives me hope. I try to hold back tears, but they stream down my face like a river breaking through a dam. Finally letting go of him shatters my heart into a thousand tiny pieces, while a whisper of solace lingers in the air between us - giving me hope that one day things will get better, even if not today.

I slowly turn around, and that's when I see them. My mother and brother are standing there, and they are both silently crying. There is something infinitely sad about them, a look of deep sadness and sorrow that I can feel even from across the room. We lock our eyes and somehow, in this moment, I know that we all understand each other.

Without saying a word, I move forward and embrace my parents in a tight hug. The unmistakable smell of the hospital clings to our clothes as we hold each other, and in this moment, the sorrow and hope of it all seem to swell around us. I feel my own tears mix with theirs, and for a moment, it truly feels like everything will be alright.

He says with eyes full of hope, "I know I can beat this. Don't worry, everything will be okay." This was the answer to the silent question that screamed in my head. His words carry the weight of optimism, a balm for the uncertainties that grip my heart.

I understand that he says this to provide comfort, but beneath his reassuring smile, the sinking feeling still lingers. In moments like these, I grasp the value of every word he speaks, realizing that each one is precious and holds the power to bring solace.

Despite the overwhelming weight of the situation, I contain my emotions, a protective shield guarding my pain. I choose to keep my worries and fears hidden, convinced that sharing my burdens would be a burden in itself. Instead, I channel my energy into offering him unwavering strength and reassurance during his darkest hours, grasping to uphold my own facade of strength. With each smile and every embrace, I communicate the unspoken words: 'I love you and I will be with you the entire way. I wish I could go through the pain and suffering with you and take away some of it."

Suppressing my feelings becomes my new reality, a necessary sacrifice to stay strong for my family. It is a role I must figure out, navigating this unfamiliar terrain with the weight of my dad's illness on my heart. He doesn't say much—just takes my hand in his and gives it a light squeeze. In that moment, some of the tension that has built within me eases, as if his touch carries a glimmer of hope. But my heart still remains heavy, burdened by the knowledge of the difficult path that lies ahead.

"Don't worry," he whispers, his voice filled with determination. "We will get through this, and we will be back home, happy once again." His words become a lifeline, a reminder to hold onto hope and persevere, even when the journey seems unbearable. And as he continues to hold my hand, I find strength in his unwavering belief, knowing that together, we are facing the challenges ahead and will emerge on the other side, stronger and filled with gratitude for every precious moment we have together.

CHAPTER THREE
Time, Tears, and Hidden Emotions

Stay with me, I silently implore, wishing desperately that he can remain by my side forever. But reality crashes upon us once again, shattering any illusion of permanence we may have and leaving my heart completely broken. My heart breaks further, becoming even more fractured and fragile. Forever broken.

Every day seems to stretch out endlessly, yet the time is never enough. It will never be enough. My family carries on, putting on a brave face, pretending that my dad's cancer is nothing more than a passing shadow. But deep down, we know the storm is brewing, ready to unleash its fury upon us at any given moment. The days of petty arguments and unspoken words are gone, replaced by an urgency to express love and affection as if each unspoken sentiment carries a ticking clock.

Hope becomes a fragile thread, slipping through my fingers just when I need it most. I need to learn to hide my sadness and my emotions from my dad. I want him to believe that everything will be okay. The last thing I want is for him to worry about me. So I bury my emotions deep within, only allowing them to resurface during solitary moments in my car, when the weight becomes too heavy to bear. But even then, the task of hiding my fear, my sadness, and the constant urge to burst into tears becomes nearly impossible. When will it get easier? How can I possibly succeed at concealing my emotions in such a short amount of time? I yearn for someone to wake me from this never-ending nightmare, to grant me a reprieve from the constant ache in my heart.

Time with my dad is a precious gift, and I feel an overwhelming urge to express all of the emotions that are bottled up inside me. Every time we meet, I am haunted by the fear that it might be the final goodbye between us, and the burden of unspoken words becomes too much to bear. Time, once a fleeting concept, now takes on a haunting presence. The past blurs into insignificance, and all that remains is the stark realization that our time together is limited. The thought suffocates me, and I long for him to be with me until the end of time. Defeat is an unbearable prospect, a nightmare that plagues my thoughts on the daily. I try to redirect my mind, to focus on something else, but it proves to be an epic failure.

At home, we anxiously await the hospital's call, knowing that it will determine the next steps for my dad's diagnosis and treatment. The conflicting thoughts swirling in my mind create a twisted way of thinking. Part of me hopes that the absence of a ringing phone signifies that his case isn't as serious as we fear, while another part whispers that the silence only confirms the grim reality of advanced cancer with little hope.

Time seems to drag on, and every passing hour intensifies the anticipation. Everyone's eyes are constantly glued to the phone as if we're certain that at any given moment, it comes alive with a shrill ringing that will bring with it a verdict of life or death. It's been a few hours since we found out about my dad's cancer diagnosis, and we anxiously await the hospital's call. I sip from a glass of water at dinner, then watch it empty in slow motion, wishing that time would pass faster, awaiting the dreaded phone call. The shrill ring of the phone echoes throughout the room, reverberating against the walls and making us all jump.

10 p.m., the phone finally rings, shattering the uneasy stillness of the room. Why do they have to call at such an hour, deviating from the regular hours of operation? Fear grips us, leaving us hesitant to answer, knowing that the message on the other end will shape my dad's future with irreversible consequences. With trembling hands, I mustered the courage to pick up the phone. It's the call we have been waiting for, the call that holds my dad's fate in its words. My heart pounds so loudly that I'm certain the hospital receptionist can hear it through the receiver. As I nervously take the call, I attempt to steady my voice to make sense of the words. But the mantra of "it is what it is" soon makes it clear what lies ahead.

I glare at the phone as it lights up in the dark, its incessant ringing shattering the silence that has engulfed us all night. I know why they are calling; I know what news they will bring with them that could shape my dad's future irrevocably. But a part of me wishes to stay in this moment, not knowing what lay ahead; if we knew, it would no longer be an uncertain future but a certain one with irreversible consequences. The notion of "no news is good news" quickly crumbles, shattering my wishful thinking of a misdiagnosis. The weight of reality presses down upon us, forcing us to confront the daunting journey ahead.

"Hello?" I ask, my voice shaking with anticipation. After what feels like an eternity, a nurse on the other end of the line finally speaks. "We have a room open for your dad on the cancer floor," she says. "You'll need to proceed to the registration area immediately to admit him."

I hang up the phone and take a few deep breaths, trying to hold back tears. "They want him to go to the hospital… now," I manage to whisper.

The words slowly settle in, weighing on me like a ton of bricks. Suddenly, everything feels like it's happening in slow motion. I can barely comprehend what is going on, my mind racing and my heart breaking. I can see the sadness in my parents' eyes. Our dream of a misdiagnosis dissolves in an instant, replaced by the crushing reality that my dad has been diagnosed correctly and must embark on the difficult road ahead. I feel my heart crumble under the weight of knowledge, overwhelmed by this unavoidable truth.

The drive to the hospital is accompanied by a sinking feeling in the pit of my stomach. The road seems to stretch like a gray ribbon on the horizon. A sickening sense of dread is heavy in my stomach as we fly over the potholes and bumps like a stone skipping over water. The drive to the hospital feels like an eternity has passed as I grind my teeth, fear consuming me. The familiar roads that have once brought us so much joy now seem to be leading us toward something ominous, something darker and more unpredictable than either of us has ever experienced.

The interior of the car is oppressive and thick with emotion, my dad's silence only adding to its heaviness. His face is etched with pain deep within, and he gives off a labored breath every few seconds while clutching his stomach. Taking his hand in mine, I squeeze it gently, a gesture of understanding, and he responds with an almost imperceptible nod and the ghost of a smile. I clasp my one free hand tightly on the steering wheel so that my knuckles turn white. The only sounds are the rhythmic hum of the engine and the occasional sniffle from myself. With each passing minute, a boulder of dread settles in my stomach, weighing me down with a sense of absolute fear. The bleak irony of this situation hits me like a ton of bricks as we pull into the hospital parking lot. My dad, renowned for his gentle kindness and charitable nature, is desperate for the aid of strangers and medical professionals to heal what ails him. As we step out of my SUV into the night air, we join hands in silent prayer and beg for strength, courage, and divine guidance.

We wait in dreary silence on the third floor of the parking garage, as if an eternity has been carved into time. My throat tightens until I can't breathe, overwhelmed with fear and anguish for what was about to unfold. The dim light gives the parking garage the feeling as if we were entering some hidden catacomb, all hope blown away. We stand staring at the doors of the elevator as if they hold some power to save us from our despair. Transport us to another dimension. Then, in a quiet hum, the elevator doors open, slicing through the oppressive stillness like a razor. We step inside and begin to descend - each passing second feeling like a year.

I turn to face the window, hoping to hold back the tears that threaten to escape as each floor takes us closer to our destination. My vision blurs and I feel a sharp pang in my chest – my heart feels like it's about to burst from my chest as I try desperately not to cry; I know that whatever awaits us will be difficult to face. Suddenly, a single tear escapes down my cheek and I cannot stop the flood of emotion that follows. Tears pour down my face, my shoulders shaking slightly with every sob. No one speaks, no one moves; all that can be heard is our collective breathing - labored and filled with despair.

Another lump forms in my throat or at this point, it is the same one that is just permanently lodged there as a constant reminder of the emotions I was desperately trying to suppress. I take a deep breath and reach for my dad's hand, seeking solace in his presence as we step into the elevator that will take us to the hospital entrance. He squeezes my hand as if to offer what little reassurance he can give me in this moment of complete sadness. Guilt washes over me as I know he is the one hurting and I fight back my tears. We stand there for an eternity, sharing grief-filled embraces until finally, the elevator stops at its destination: the ground floor of the parking garage.

Stepping out of the elevator, we are greeted by the revolving doors, serving as a physical divide between the nightmare that awaits us and the world we once knew, where everything is normal. My heart pounds as we walk through those doors, entering a place where hope and faith seem so far away. The stark white walls offer no comfort or reassurance as I focus on putting one foot in front of the other right behind his slow and painful footsteps.

Walking hand in hand, my mom on one side of my dad and me on the other, we make our way through the revolving doors. We are immediately assaulted by the antiseptic odor and a hum of activity that persists despite the late hour. To our immediate right is the cafe, bustling with people getting food during their stay. On the left side, a partition with empty chairs lined against the walls provides an oasis of solitude during chaos. The hospital's interior lacks warmth and inviting colors, an oversight that only adds to the overall dreariness of the environment. The buzzing fluorescent lights seem to emphasize the urgency of the situation, but despite the loud voices and busyness of the hospital's main floor, we feel strangely alone, isolated from the rest of the hospital goers.

The information desk, in its dark brown hue, blends in with the somber palette of the hospital, highlighting the lack of vibrancy and hope that seems to permeate the atmosphere. There is no warmth or inviting colors to greet us, only dark hues and bleakness. We wait in line for what seems like an eternity before finally reaching the front, where a polite young woman answers our inquiries and nods her head to a machine that will dispense a number and informs us that we will be called to the desk and to make our way to the waiting area for registration. We then continue down the main entrance hallway, which is painted in an uninspiring shade of gray. Everywhere we look, people are moving up and down the hallways dressed in hospital gowns, pushing IV poles, and wearing bright blue non-slip socks. The stark contrast between their attire and the dreary surroundings stands out as a reminder that this is our new reality.

An intense pain grips my chest, constricting my breath as I navigate through the hospital toward the registration area. The walls seem to close in on me, suffocating me with a sense of overwhelming despair. But I can't let myself give up or break down; I must keep going, one step at a time. My dad is probably feeling just helpless and broken—perhaps even worse off than I am—but I know we have to keep believing that things will get better.

I can't help but feel a heavy sadness for my dad, who is struggling with his illness while still trying to put on a brave face. It's painful to watch him pretending everything is alright when inside he must be so scared. I'm too afraid to even ask him how he feels; I know I wouldn't be able to handle the answer. If only there were something, anything I could do to make this all go away. I know that he is hiding how much pain he is really in from us all.

As my dad pulls a ticket from the dispenser, we all gather by his side. People shuffle forward one number at a time to desks that are each sectioned off. A woman is standing behind a desk, calling people forward repeatedly; she's so focused on what she's doing that she doesn't even notice us there. This place, this hospital, feels detached from the compassion and care it should provide – just another place of business. These feelings shouldn't consume anyone who walks through these doors. Even though the waiting room is relatively empty, the lack of personalized attention only intensifies my frustration and fear. It's as if the hospital has adopted a system relative to the impersonal nature of the DMV, where patients are reduced to mere numbers in a queue. My momentary anger may seem petty in the grand scheme of things, but it's a desperate attempt to alleviate my pain and create a distraction. Any distraction will do.

A deep silence lingers in the air as the nurse finally calls out his number. He shuffles forward, pale face lined with worry, to receive the blue wrist tag that confirms his registration as a patient. I clutch the stack of paperwork tightly in my hands, feeling a crushing heaviness at its weight. It carries a long list of requirements—proof of finances, work experience, medical history and so many more forms demanding personal details of endless information.

This is my task for the night, my own personal homework, as we're directed to the 7th floor of the hospital—the cancer ward where he'll now reside.

A nurse comes to escort us to his room. We follow her through long corridors that lead us to several elevators. We slowly enter an elevator, and the doors close behind us. There's a noticeable chill in the air as we ascend to the seventh floor—the cancer ward. His new address for an "x" amount of time – now let's solve for "x." No, this problem needs to be left alone as I do not want to know.

As we make our way to the designated floor, the gravity of the situation settles deeper within me. There's no turning back now, and the ache in my chest intensifies as if the weight of the world rests upon it. The pain is so overwhelming, it feels as though it could consume me entirely. The hallways we pass are so convoluted that I can barely remember how we even got to the first set of elevators let alone this path leading to the second set. The elevator is empty and fluorescently lit; as soon as we step inside and push the button, we're surrounded by barely controlled chaos. The elevator doors slide open with a loud creak, revealing a waiting area filled with chairs and two metal doors that are open, revealing a long hallway lined with white walls.

I take a deep breath before stepping off, bracing myself for the unknown. I'm torn between anger at my circumstances and sadness at what they might mean for our future. I'm overwhelmed by a strange feeling of dread as if I'm entering another world entirely separate from the one we just left behind. We step out into a much different atmosphere than before; it is colder and eerily quiet, drenched in sterility that stings in my nostrils like straight alcohol. I can feel a palpable tension emanating from the walls of this cancer ward.

Please, I silently plead, help me find the strength to keep breathing through this anguish. I'm terrified of losing him, the person I cherish most in this world. Watching him slip away right before my eyes is an indescribable agony. There are moments when I wish time would stop, so we can make the most of the time we have together. But with every passing minute, the pressure of grief keeps increasing and intensifying in my heart. I don't know where this road will lead; however, even if it's too hard, I won't let him go through this journey without me. I'm scared, absolutely terrified of what lies ahead, but I cannot bear to see him suffer alone.

CHAPTER FOUR
A New Address: 7th Floor — Room 701

7th Floor – the cancer floor – our new address

At this late hour, the seventh floor lies in dark and quiet repose. The lights have been dimmed; their glow swallowed by the shadows. The hallways have a few individuals, their bodies adorned with IV lines and various tubes, bearing the visible marks of their courageous fight against chemotherapy and radiation. The absence of hair on many of their heads stands as a testament to the hardships they have endured.

Suppressing the torrents of tears that threaten to overflow from my eyes and engulf my shattered heart, I muster a smile, a facade I wear for my dad's sake. Yet, in the depths of my being, I recognize the futility of the battle I wage against my own emotions, realizing that they will inevitably consume me sooner than later. Every part of me feels like it's screaming to turn around and flee, but I keep on going.

Tears: 10,000 vs. Hiding emotions: 0.

We move down the hallway just a few feet away from the main lounge area of the floor, with the double doors wide open. With every step we take, my heart starts to beat faster, and I find myself frozen in place as if my body knows what awaits us ahead. The smell of the hospital is cloying and suffocating, like something between stale air, metal, and sickness. It's a cloying smell that feels as if it is suffocating you. There is a faint smell of disinfectant, perhaps from the hospital corridors. I could almost feel the illness in the air, as if the very walls themselves were steeped in sadness, despair, and pain. Taking a moment to gather myself before entering, I steel myself for what lies ahead: uncertainty, death, and anything else that cancer seemed to bring along -- things that no one should ever have to face alone. We follow the nurse silently as she leads us down the hallway, then pauses in front of a door marked 'Room 701.'

The answer to "x" is staring me in my face. With a fake smile and a trembling hand, I reach for the door handle to room 701 – wishing that this was an entry into another dimension. I'll take any dimension at this rate. Just not the current one.

Within the confines of his hospital room, my dad shares his space with another patient, the flimsy curtain serving as a feeble divider, failing to offer any semblance of privacy. As he looks towards my mother, then shifts his gaze towards me, his words resonate with unwavering faith, assuring us, "Don't worry, everything is in God's hands. I won't be staying here long. I will beat this and come home soon." I pray for the strength to shield him from the emotions that are always threatening to overwhelm me, and the ever-present lump that may as well be permanently lodged in my throat that serves as a constant reminder of the gravity of the situation.

The desire to believe in those comforting words tugs at every fiber of my being, yet an undercurrent of terror still grips my heart, refusing to relinquish its hold. The weight of the word 'cancer' hangs heavy in my thoughts, a shared experience for so many, yet when it strikes someone so close, its gravity takes on a newfound intensity. The survival rates for Stage IV are starkly known to be low, and the importance of early detection echoes through my mind.

My dad had been complaining of unusual fatigue and abdominal pain for months. He had gone to multiple doctors, but every test came back negative. Finally, after a year of searching for an answer, he was diagnosed with Hepatitis. In his case, early detection was not even a possibility, as he endured a misdiagnosis and a year-long treatment for Hepatitis and acid reflux. Now his already compromised body was being weakened even further.

He attempts to maintain a lighthearted facade to spare us from further pain, yet an ominous feeling fills my chest as I realize that our suffering has only just begun. He puts on a brave face, but I can see the fear in his eyes as we enter this uncertain future together.

As we try to get my dad comfortable in the hospital room, seeking some semblance of comfort for my dad amidst the unknown duration of his stay, I settle myself at the edge of his bed, attempting to inject moments of levity into the heavy atmosphere. Yet, concealing the anguish that gnaws at my insides proves an arduous task.

How can I possibly navigate through this? How am I going to have the courage to keep going? In the silence that envelops the room, the only respite lies in taking it one minute at a time. The thought of my dad being alone, surrounded by the steady hum of machines, fills me with unease. I want nothing more than for him to be surrounded by my mom during these dark times. But at the same time, deep down, I know that our financial situation prevents us from getting him the private room he needs. How can I reconcile these two realities?

Never could I have fathomed that we would be facing this harrowing ordeal, finding ourselves admitted to a floor dedicated to those battling cancer. Why must our path diverge so drastically? It feels as though I am trapped in a suffocating corner, devoid of escape. How do I summon the strength to wear a facade of lightheartedness, to be a pillar of strength for my dad, while the weight of my own emotions threatens to consume me? Is this the onset of the final chapter, the beginning of the end?

I wish someone would help me. Just breathe. This is the only thing I can keep telling myself.

Within the confines of the room, a sparse arrangement greeted my eyes. A solitary television hung at the center, meant to be shared by both patients, casting a faint glow across the room. A small dresser held an enigmatic monitoring device, its purpose eluding me, while a lone reclining chair stood adjacent to a modest sink. Adorning the wall beside the entrance, a plastic holder housed three boxes of McKesson gloves, each in varying sizes, alongside a can of foam hand sanitizer. The ambiance of this place felt devoid of warmth, an uninviting and somber environment. Yet, paradoxically, it held the potential to offer us a glimmer of hope amidst the despair. To the side, a diminutive window offered a meager view, rendering the vast expanse of the sky an elusive sight. Instead, the side that my dad was on captured the perpetual motion of nurses and doctors scurrying along the hallway.

Stepping outside into the corridor, I caught sight of a small refrigerator housing tiny apple juice boxes, its top doubling as an ice maker. Amidst the bleakness, a sliver of positivity emerged—is this considered the silver lining that people spoke of, or am I just delusional given the circumstances? I was grateful that he was situated close to the ice maker, enabling me to readily fetch him cold refreshments, should he ask. Dear God, let him stay alive. I am willing to do anything, as long as he is okay. Grant me a wish that he will be okay or take me instead. I choose the first, but I'll settle for the latter.

Ice maker: my silver lining

Heart: shattered and barely held together

This must be what it is to be desperate to grasp anything that can reflect any glimmer of hope or any outlet to escape the pain and the reality of the current situation. Either that or I am losing my mind. At this point, the only option left was to accept that hopelessness is now my only reality.

I stand frozen next to the hospital bed, my eyes locked on the two doctors who have just entered the room. As if framed by a spotlight, they stand illuminated beneath the white light radiating from the window, dressed in white jackets and stethoscopes draped around their necks. As if I had stepped into a Dr. Seuss book, I see Thing 1 and Thing 2, two doctors with name tags pinned to their left chests - Dr. One, a first-year resident, and Dr. Two, a third-year resident, respectively. They politely introduce themselves in unison and begin to explain their roles in the medical staff. Their names elude me along with everything else.

My dad sits up, his pain-filled voice resonating through the room. "Hello, I'm Pastor Kim," he said with a smile, extending a friendly handshake to the two doctors.

The two doctors, taken aback by my dad's fluency in English, quickly inquire as to how he acquired such proficiency at his age. I feel a momentary pang of anger as I wonder why anyone would be astonished by an Asian person speaking English fluently in America. It feels discourteous, just outright rude and ignorant. I am briefly lost in my thoughts before the doctors return their attention to me and my dad.

As my dad proceeds to explain that he earned his doctorate at Southwestern Theological Seminary in 1985, the doctors express their admiration. Really? Am I truly listening to them discuss their amazement at a foreigner attaining an academic achievement? Does discrimination persist even in such moments? Annoyance surges within me. While any diversion from the current situation may be welcome, this particular topic seems strikingly out of place. Finally, they refocus on the matter at hand, delving into the next steps which involve conducting further tests and biopsies, from which they will proceed accordingly. And with that final note, both of us were left alone in our hospital room awaiting test results while reflecting upon our conversation with the two doctors. My eyes followed them as they stepped out into the hallway with their white jackets swaying side-to-side behind them like shadows in the night – Dr. Thing 1 and Dr. Thing 2 on their way out of sight...

After enduring a series of jabs, or perhaps they are escalating to painful stabs by now, the distinction between the two seems irrelevant in this moment of torment. The line between jabs and stabs has been blurred long ago; all he can focus on is the intensity of his suffering.

A different doctor comes to explain the results of the biopsies, delivering a mixture of relief and concern. The findings reveal minimal traces of cancer on the exterior of his stomach, along with two small tumors on his liver, while no signs of cancer are detected in his bones. The edges of his lips turn up in relief when he sees "no signs of cancer detected in bones" scribbled onto the paper. Worry creases his forehead when he reads the diagnosis of small tumors on his liver, and a twinge of fear runs through me as I realize that the cancer is slowly spreading in his body. The absence of cancer in his bones brings a momentary breath of relief, indicating that the disease has not spread to such a critical extent.

However, the presence of the two tumors on his liver sent a chill down my spine, a sobering reminder of the daunting battle ahead. Any fragment of positive news, however slight, offered a glimmer of hope amidst the relentless onslaught of adversity. The doctor cautioned that although the existing liver spots remained relatively small, it was only a matter of time before the cancer might proliferate and extend its reach to his lungs. The substantial amount of cancer present in his stomach posed a daunting challenge, prompting the medical team to proceed with caution in their treatment approach, and surgery was not an option.

CHAPTER FIVE
Hope or Surrender

Among the options presented to us, two paths emerged, each fraught with its significant consequences. One path extends his life for a few months while the other could lead to a fate even worse.

Option 1: Chemotherapy, to impede the spread of the cancer, holding onto the glimmer of hope that it might diminish the disease or, at the very least, sustain its current state. It stands as a daunting endeavor, requiring resilience and endurance of the side effects with uncertain outcomes and absolutely no guarantees.

Option 2: A choice that carries the weight of a somber pronouncement - to provide medications solely aimed at alleviating discomfort and enhancing the quality of life. Accepting the stark reality that this path may lead to a peaceful passing. This just seems to highlight the inevitable nature of mortality that I am not ready to face.

Teetering on the edge of an abyss, wracked with indecision with the weight of two choices. The tension between hope and acceptance, or the testing of resilience, hangs over us like a deluge, threatening to drown us with one wrong decision. I sit, divided between two paths: neither one entirely safe. The weight of the decision is almost unbearable as if we are holding a double-edged sword, each sharp enough to cut deep regardless of which side is held. No matter what we choose, the pain will be deep and enduring. It feels like hope is trying to fight acceptance, and resilience battling surrender – it seems impossible to decide between them. As I am unable to predict the outcome that would come of either choice.

My mom tells me to ask the doctor what he would do. As if on cue, the minute I turn to ask the doctor what he recommends: without any hesitation, he responds with option 2.

"No," we all say simultaneously. His choice echoes finality, as if waiting is the only option.

The weight of the decision to forgo active treatment and instead focus on making him comfortable until his passing looms heavily upon us. It feels like a choice steeped in resignation, an admission of defeat, and an acceptance of the imminent loss that awaits us. How can we simply relinquish all hope and surrender to the impending reality of death? The notion seems inconceivable, as my mom's only option was to explore any possibility that could potentially extend his life. In agreement, my dad nods, ready to initiate the challenging course of chemotherapy.

The die is cast, and there is no turning back. The harrowing truth of our decision sinks in, dragging us into a pit of terror and dread. My entire being is wracked with fear and anxiety as we take this treacherous plunge into the unknown. Our every movement seems to be fraught with danger and consequences, leaving us with no choice but to bravely march forward despite our doubts and trepidation. We grasp onto the faintest shreds of hope that cling to the air like smoke, desperately praying that our chosen path will lead us to the most favorable outcome.

Overwhelmed by the weight of the news and the impending fate that hangs heavily over his life, I find myself stepping out of the room. Tears stream down my face, an outpouring that matches the turmoil within my heart. The sheer intensity of it all compresses my heart, constricting my breath and leaving me gasping for air. At this moment, I wish for time to stand still. The unrelenting torrent of emotions keeps coming, a relentless ache that permeates every fiber of my being. I move silently down the hallway, casting a glance back at my dad's hospital door. I have seen the look of defeat in his eyes after hearing the only option that we had with not much hope. I know that one way or another he is doomed - and I can do nothing to save him. I need an escape for a moment.

For a while, I simply stand there, lost in my thoughts, until I feel a pair of hands clasping my shoulders. I turn around to see my mother standing behind me, her eyes brimming with tears. "What do we do?" she barely whispers. I have no answers. I don't even know if we are making the right choice.

I wish there existed a manual, a comprehensive guide specifically crafted for families thrust into the intricate web of cancer. The realm of scientific terminologies and complex medical procedures feels like an insurmountable mountain, one that I struggle to climb. I am hoping that my dad will be assigned to a compassionate oncologist who will simplify and demystify the jargon, allowing me to grasp the intricacies with clarity. However, whether I will fully accept and comprehend the information presented to me remains a separate challenge altogether. The magnitude of this ordeal tests the limits of my capacity to absorb and understand; the enormity of this ordeal feels even more overwhelming.

Fighting back tears, I steel myself to wear a fake smile and re-enter his sterile room, where the nurse had already arrived with a lukewarm dinner. Plastic trays piled high with what could only be described as hospital food: a wheat roll dense enough to double as a paperweight, chicken so overcooked it was practically sawdust, and mashed potatoes that looked more like flakes rather than real potatoes. The one redeeming dish on the tray is a tepid bowl of chicken noodle soup. It smells of home and comfort but is still flavorless – all we have left are these bland imitations.

As I take the tray from the nurse and place it in front of him, I see the anticipation in his eyes. He tries to hide it, but I know he hopes for something full of flavor. Opening the plastic fork and spoon, I cautiously take a bite of food. The chicken is rubbery and flavorless - clearly unseasoned - and I can feel my heart sink. How could anyone be expected to eat this?

Looking across at my dad, who is already waiting eagerly for me to finish my test bite, I give him some encouragement. "Surprisingly, it's not as bad as it looks," I say with more conviction than I feel. Without complaint, he eats every bite without pause. As he chokes down the bland chicken and dry roll, I can see his hunger after waiting all day in the hospital. He takes a hesitant bite of the bland-tasting chicken and struggles to find something savory to focus on. Convincing myself that this meal is essential for his recovery, I urge him to eat every bite. Even though the unseasoned chicken tastes like rubber and the wheat roll is hard and dry, without a single complaint from my dad, he forces himself to swallow each bite. Despite the unpalatable taste, he continues to eat until the tray is empty.

I clench my fists as tears stream down my face. "I'm so sorry, Daddy," I sob, feeling the weight of our impending future bear down on me like a crushing force. My own need to help him drive away his pain is clouded with selfishness that twists within me, wanting his suffering to simply stop. I understand that this battle will be long and difficult, but all I want is for him to tell me everything will be alright.

I force myself to look into his eyes, searching for the strength that usually resides there. Instead, I see fear and vulnerability peeking out from behind his mask of reassurance. My heart drops to the pit of my stomach as I realize the gravity of my dad's illness. His attempt at a smile breaks my heart as the pain radiates from him, mixing with my own fear, grief, longing, and vulnerability until I'm shaking uncontrollably. His pain is more than evident in his expression as he struggles to keep up a strong facade for me. I can almost feel his fear, grief, longing, and vulnerability radiating off him through his trembling hands that I grasp tightly, silently praying for his recovery.

I wrap my arms around him and hug him tight, wanting to take away some of his suffering. The reality of our situation hits hard—there is no cure for what he's going through. All we can do is face it together and make the best out of whatever time we have left.

"Someone help me," I struggle to hold back the tears that well up within me, threatening to spill over at any given moment. A kind nurse with warm eyes and a compassionate smile enters the room as if on cue. She offers me the opportunity to stay with my dad overnight so that I could be there when his oncologist makes her rounds. She warns us to stay put in the room, though, as others may not understand why she allowed such an exception. Her gentle voice wraps itself around me like a comforting embrace, bringing me some much-needed peace.

He smiles as he seems relieved that I will be there for the night. He takes a deep breath and whispers, "I am okay." Those three words echo in my head, taking on an entirely new meaning now that I understand how precious time is — quality time with my dad whom I am going to miss more than anything else in the world. I feel a wave of emotions—fear for what will soon be lost, sadness for what must be endured, and love for my dad who has given so much to me over the years.

"Fighting! I love you! I'll see you tomorrow!"

CHAPTER SIX
Doctor Midnight

The old torn-up leather chair next to his hospital bed is becoming an extension of me at this point. Pieces of the armrest are so worn that I can feel the splinters stabbing my skin, only intensifying as I shift in agitation. With a trembling hand, I reach out and barely touch his hand -- all bruised and swollen from the IVs with tubes conjoined to one another as if he's trapped. His face is peaceful, masking the pain he keeps hidden from me.

I tell stories trying to keep his spirits up, and he chuckles intermittently in a way that holds none of his usual good humor. The familiar smell of the hospital is now all too familiar – the odors of medication, cleaning solutions, and sickness clinging to the air. We share an understanding gaze - one that speaks of all the changes that have occurred since he was admitted. I can't shake the feeling that these moments will soon be only memories. Already, a feeling of deep sorrow wells up inside me as I clutch his hand in mine. The magnitude of how much everything changes is completely overwhelming. I know these moments will forever be imprinted in my memory. The weight of missing him is already consuming me, even though he is physically present in the bed beside me. I can't even close my eyes for a few minutes without feeling an emptiness so deep that it might as well consume me from within

I sit beside him in the cold, worn-out leather chair next to his hospital bed. His breaths were labored and shallow, and his eyes were closed. Tears brimmed in my eyes as I thought about how he had to go through such excruciating pain. Cancer is such a mystery that causes so much pain that no human should ever have to endure. I am left unable to comprehend the pain he must be feeling. His face was gaunt and pale, a stark contrast to the jovial man I had known all my life. I want to be strong for him — to let him know that he wasn't alone — but it felt like an avalanche of sorrows was crashing down on me. How can I ever fill the deep void that would remain if he were gone? My mind raced with thousands of questions I'd never have answered, my heart screamed for strength, and yet all these powerful emotions just seemed too overwhelming.

But then there are moments when the darkness envelops me entirely. It feels like I'm being swallowed whole by this sorrowful emotion, making it hard to breathe or think straight. No amount of reassurance or distraction can bring me out of it - nothing seems to make a difference anymore.

The doctor on duty steps into the dimly lit room waking us up close to midnight. She introduces herself as his primary oncologist and that she will be the main point of contact. Her white lab coat cuts a stark contrast against the shadows. She looks at my dad and smiles warmly in a way that is clearly meant to put him at ease and yet inspire respect. "How's your pain? On a scale from 1 to 10?" she asks softly but knowingly. He looks away, forces a smile, and says, "Zero. I do not feel pain at all right now." His tone contains a hint of sadness and resignation, and I feel a wave of fear.

The nurse speaks slowly, her voice gentle and even. She looks through the thick medical chart for the results from his blood lab test earlier that day. Her eyes scan over the papers as she starts reciting numbers to the doctor. Satisfied with what she sees, she nods solemnly in our direction and says everything appears to be stable. She adds that if his numbers stay consistent for another week, she mentions the possibility of him being discharged soon. Dr. Midnight then steps forward, painting an easier-to-understand picture of what it all means, making sure we understand without any confusion. She proceeds to explain the blood test results in more detail. She points out that his white and red blood cell counts are both lower than normal but still within a safe range. She also suggests that we continue to monitor it closely, as there is still a risk of infection, and if he gets sick everything will have to be pushed out.

The doctor describes the concept of chemotherapy in detail, explaining how it works by targeting and destroying cancer cells in the body while minimizing its impact on healthy cells. Despite its potential benefits, she cautions us about its side effects such as nausea and hair loss. The doctor supports her explanation by recommending that they start with low doses of chemotherapy to assess his body's reaction before gradually increasing it if necessary.

She gives us comfort and hope by assuring us that things are looking good so far and expressing her optimism for my dad's recovery. We feel reassured by her kind words, despite not knowing for sure how things will turn out in the end. My mother thanks the nurse sincerely for her thoughtful advice and support.

My daily life revolves solely around the hospital. Every morning, I struggle to drive to work as every minute feels like a countdown until I can see my dad again. My car feels like a time machine pulling me through an alternate universe, away from my dad. Tears force themselves out of my eyes with each passing second, pouring down my face on the way to and from work as it is almost a relief to know no one sees them. This is my only chance to let go and cry without worrying about how it would make my dad sad to see me this way. Every journey to the hospital feels like it could be my last, so I cling to each moment desperately hoping for another tomorrow.

Work in itself is a distraction. However, someone always asks about my situation and can sense the underlying sadness in me. I'm losing myself. I work, but my mind is elsewhere. It's on him, and the better part of my days are spent thinking and rethinking. I am consumed by doubt and regret masking my sadness. I become blank and muted when asked how I am doing; the words linger in the air like a soft sigh. "Are you okay?" fades away into a far-off echo. The simple question seems impossible to answer anymore because it has the power to unleash a torrent of emotions within me. If I try to avoid answering. I seem cold and distant. I appear okay when I am only trying not to give in to all the emotions that are about to swallow me whole. My attempt to conceal my emotions only makes it more difficult for me.

The days slowly pass by, and all of them blend into an indistinguishable blur. The only thing that keeps me going through this tough time is being able to go back to the hospital and see my dad as soon as possible at the end of each workday. As much as I dread having to leave him every night, knowing that I will get to see him again soon gives me hope and propels me forward.

Sleep eludes me as the fear of losing him takes hold. I am merely existing, functioning in a zombie-like state. The drive to the hospital after work becomes a meltdown of tears and silent prayers. How can one person cry so relentlessly? I hope that tears will eventually run dry, but they seem infinite. In the hospital parking garage, I hurriedly touched up my makeup, concealing my tear-stained face. With a forced smile and a deep breath, I suppress any tears threatening to escape as I ascend to his room.

As I walk down the hallway, I notice a faint smell of antiseptic in the air and hear the sound of beeps from medical equipment that getting louder the closer I get to his room. The dull floor makes my steps echo all around me, bouncing off the walls with a hollow ring that falls into nothingness. There is so little here to break the monotony of this long corridor. I quickly scan the hallway to see if he is out and about walking with the other patients. He is nowhere to be seen, so I slowly make my way down the long corridor, passing patients and visitors on the way. I pause for a moment to lean against the cold wall, closing my eyes in preparation before pushing open the door to his room. As I round the corner of the curtain that is drawn, I see him, lying in his bed, eyes closed but he is still breathing. I glance at the oxygen sensor and the heart rate monitor that was as steady as a metronome. Perfect and steady. His appearance has drastically changed over the last few days, and as I approach him, my heart sinks. He looks so tired and so frail; this is tearing his body up.

In those precious moments of daily sadness, a profound calm envelops me upon seeing my dad's smile. The emotional emptiness that consumes me seems to dissipate, if only briefly, as he holds my hand and beams at me as if he has been waiting all day for me to come.

CHAPTER SEVEN
10 Days: Hiding Tears, Holding Hope

The incessant beeping of machines fills the background, acting as a comforting metronome. Each pulse reassures me that, for now at least, everything is okay, though that could change without warning. What was once an obnoxious noise has become a necessity, calming my nerves and providing a semblance of peace—just white noise. The air hangs thick with an unusual stillness as if the chaos that led us here has momentarily paused. Despite the seriousness of my dad's condition, a strange calm settles over me in the golden rays of sunlight streaming through the window. My heart rate slows, my breath steadies, and my mind clears. In this moment of clarity, I feel an unexpected strength; maybe I can face anything.

Approaching the bedside, I meet my dad's eyes as he weakly smiles. Taking his hand, warmth spreads from his skin into mine, creating a sense of peace between us. I feel as if he will beat this, or I keep telling myself that if he says he will, then it must be true. I know I'm holding my breath all the time, but this is painful. I just want him here. I'm hurting over all these sad days, but I'm ok as he's still right beside me. I still believe him when he says he will be ok.

A nurse wheels in a dinner tray, complete with steaming vegetables and some overcooked pieces of meat. My anxiety prevents me from eating, but I force myself to take a few bites as his "taste tester." The steak is heavy and tough under my fork, like chewing leather or swallowing a tire. My dad watches me eat, waiting for me to say it's "pretty good," then starts to scoop out his portions, savoring each bite. If only I could bring in my mom's home-cooked meal, but the nurse had strictly advised maintaining his diet according to the doctor's orders. We talk about anything other than his illness, work, and what the future will hold as if he will always be there.

My dad and I spend a lot of time walking the hospital halls, using his IV pole as an opportunity to escape the monotony of the room. We explore and take in the sights and sounds of a hospital filled with strangers, some just admitted and others preparing for discharge.

Encountering patients in worse situations than my dad's is bittersweet. It humbles us, bringing us closer together and showing us how lucky we are to have each other despite his illness.

We also witness heartwarming moments when patients, declared cancer-free, announce their victories. It's as if overcoming the initial hospital stay is the only hurdle to face. Those walks become part of our daily routine, reminding us that life can be beautiful even in trying times. They give my dad hope when all seems lost, and I feel like he'll always be with me.

Time slips away during our daily chats and walks around the cancer floor. The stillness of the atmosphere becomes the norm. Scuff marks and fingerprints tell stories on the white walls, and the beeping monitors offer a strangely peaceful sound. Constant and steady beeps signify that life is still present.

As visitation time nears its end, tears always seem to arrive at the perfect moment. My heart feels torn knowing I'll have to leave him while he peacefully drifts off to sleep. The nurses notice my lingering, but they never rush me to leave right at 10 p.m. Every day, I'm by his bedside, holding his hand and never wanting to let go. Leaving is scary, as my only thought is that I hope he wakes up tomorrow.

The idea of laughing again without feeling searing pain paralyzes my mind. My dad, my protector, now needs my care. I'm determined that as long as I keep him close, nothing in this world will break me. Reality has its cruel ways, and I wish with all my heart that this is just a nightmare, one I can awaken from soon. I wish something would take this pain away.

Meanwhile, my dad's daily routine revolves around reactions to medication and managing pain levels. Connected to an IV for fluids and another IV for additional medications, he endures intermittent pokes and blood draws throughout the day. The Midnight Doctor, almost omnipresent, makes multiple visits to check his vital signs. She's become a part of our lives, always there when needed. It doesn't matter what time it is; she tirelessly makes her rounds, sometimes even at 2 a.m. When I stay overnight with him, my bed is a leather chair, and I jump at the voice of the doctor, who just smiles at me curled up beside his bed, holding his hand. She offers a glimmer of hope in our darkest moments, treating my dad not as a statistic but as a person whose life is worth saving.

Arriving at the hospital after work fills me with nervous anticipation—the only time I look forward to throughout the day but also fear the most. The uncertainty of my dad's condition keeps me on edge, holding my breath from the moment I enter the parking garage until the elevator doors open on his floor. As I pull into the parking garage, my hands tighten on the steering wheel, and my heart races against my chest. The concrete walls amplify the screeching of tires as they echo off the cold stone. Riding the elevator up, the image of him lying motionless refuses to leave my mind.

Sprinting down the hallway to his room, my heart pounds. Will I find him better, or will this be the moment when everything changes for the worse? My mind refuses to even contemplate what that might mean. Every desperate step brings me closer to the unknown, my thoughts swirling with dread and questions. All I do is hold my breath every time I reach to open his door and pray silently that he is still alive. Please be alive. I stagger down the hallway towards what is supposed to be my refuge, only to be met by a horrific sight. My dad lies in front of me, grey and gaunt, features cast with an unearthly pallor as if death itself has visited him. I feel my heart lurch as if it would stop beating at any second. It seems like cancer has come to claim him at record speed since his diagnosis just days before. Tears brim as I face the tragedy of which I am powerless to stop.

The doctor on duty and a nurse immediately entered the room, taking a thorough look at my dad's chart. She informs both me and the nurse that his blood levels are low and that they will need to administer two bags of blood, along with additional nutrients, through his IV to improve his condition. As she speaks, a glimmer of hope emerges, knowing that these interventions have the potential to alleviate his suffering and provide some relief. I know that today will be a day in which our walk will not happen.

No matter the physical pain and mental anguish, my dad's face still bears a faint smile. My dad bravely endured a transfusion of two bags of blood, never uttering a single complaint. After two hours, I'm held in suspended relief as two bags of blood slowly fill his veins with life, and color starts to return to his face, reflecting a hidden glimmer of hope in the room. Though relief is palpable, I can tell he's still in pain when he starts pressing the morphine drip button prematurely. My stomach clenches when, despite his pleas for quicker release from suffering, the nurse refuses him medication, insisting he wait exactly four hours between doses. The three-and-a-half-hour mark seemed to be the time in which it would wear off. Each time, the nurse denies him more medication, and his desperation is palpable. Every minute feels like an eternity, and I'm rendered helpless in the face of this unfair battle.

Despite the difficulties, my dad never lets on about his struggles. As visiting hours end at 10 pm, I prepare to leave. Turning to him with a forced smile and not wanting to leave, I tell him, "I love you, Daddy! Keep fighting! Get some rest and get stronger! I'll be back tomorrow!" His face looks so sad when I tell him it's time for me to leave.

My heart breaks some more. Please, let there be a tomorrow.

Having never been apart, I ask the doctor for an exception, allowing my mom to stay with my dad past visiting hours. Thankfully, she approved. I immediately call my mom and tell her to hurry and come to the hospital for the night. From the moment he was admitted to the day of his release, which felt like an eternity, my mom remained faithfully by his side when they permitted. For ten long days, she sits in an uncomfortable chair next to him, holding his hand, praying for him, and eventually drifting off to sleep. The discomfort of the chair seems inconsequential to her if she can be there beside him. Nothing else matters.

Every night, my dad makes his rounds, determined to get his much-needed exercise. With his IV stand in tow, I accompany him, cheering him on and walking alongside him to get my own steps in. The sight of patients on each floor, walking with purpose, becomes my new reality.

For ten days, the tears come with such force that my eyes feel like they are being gouged out of my head. I lean my forehead against the cool window, trying to push back onto the pillow of glass and breathe in deeply.

Lunchtime at work is my only escape from the sea of torment and loneliness, but Cicely and Chandra come to my side like angels sent from the heavens; their presence an unspoken gesture of comfort I was not aware that I needed. We sit together in silence; no words are needed – we all know they aren't enough to heal my brokenness. As I get into my car, they can sense the approaching storm, and they hold me tight as the deluge of tears washes over me - wave after brutal wave that leaves me gasping for air. My tears are an unending torrent that soaks my cheeks until they ache, and no more liquid can be squeezed out of my swollen eyes. Despite being shattered inside, they help me hold myself together even when life feels impossible. They are not mere angels walking on earth with me; they are like my sisters fighting alongside me.

He made it! I can hardly believe it - after ten harrowing days, the hospital declared my father's cancer stable and granted us permission to take him home. But I know this is just a small break on the long and exhausting journey ahead - we still have chemotherapy treatments looming in the future. Dr. Midnight informs us that my dad will be scheduled for his first visit to the Cancer Center next week. A wave of relief washes over me; however, I also feel an oncoming dread; somehow, we mustered enough strength to survive these first ten days of uncertainty, fear, and anxiety - but what about all the ones afterward? We leave the hospital with bags full of medicine bottles that are essential for my father's battle against cancer - yet all I can think about is how bright a flicker of hope now glows against a sea of darkness.

CHAPTER EIGHT
A Brave Beginning: First Chemo Treatment

Chemotherapy - what does it entail? How will it go? There is no turning back at this point, but the anticipation of what is to come fills me with nerves. Surprisingly, the ten days in the hospital have gone relatively well. My dad only experiences flu-like symptoms and extreme exhaustion, while the pain remains manageable, and his attitude remains positive. Given the circumstances, things seem to be looking up as much as they can.

Summoning whatever hope and faith I have left; we are now embarking on his chemotherapy sessions and countless visits to the hospital. At 64 years old, the doctor has deemed my dad too old and weak for radiation treatment, and due to the cancer being at stage 4, chemotherapy is the only option. He appears ready to face whatever comes his way, while I feel like a ticking time bomb, ready to burst into tears at any given moment. He has always been my rock, the one I can rely on unwaveringly, but now the "what if" scenarios loom over me, endlessly terrifying. I know he will listen and understand, but how can I possibly convey the depth of my fear? Now it is my turn to be strong for him, no matter how weak I feel inside.

As we enter the Cancer Center, I grip my dad's hand tightly as we find our seats in the crowded waiting room. The realization hits me that this is now our reality, and there is no turning back. With his head held high and his faith unwavering, my dad walks confidently to the front desk to sign in and complete the registration form. Meanwhile, my nerves are overwhelming, and my hands tremble uncontrollably. Anxiety threatens to make me sick to my stomach.

In the Cancer Center, there are two doors on opposite ends. The one on the right leads to the doctor's office and examination rooms. On the left, a door opens as a patient emerges, revealing a row of reclining chairs, each occupied by patients connected to IV machines with bags of medicine flowing into their veins. Peering forward, I hope against hope that when my dad's name is called, someone will declare this all a terrible mistake, and we can escape from this recurring nightmare that seems to haunt every moment I close my eyes. Waking up is no escape; it's just a continuation of the nightmare.

It feels surreal to witness all the people in the cancer center, knowing that each one of them is here because they have cancer. One person in particular catches my attention—a young bald man, accompanied by his dad, and carrying a baby carrier. A soft cry emanates from the carrier, and the young man gently lifts a tiny baby, tears streaming down his face as he attempts to comfort the child. The sight is heart-wrenching. Everyone in this place is on the same path as us, facing the relentless challenge of cancer, doing whatever it takes to survive, and trying to stay strong while the disease slowly erodes their well-being. It's a constant race against time. The fear of when I will have to say goodbye looms over me, terrifying and overwhelming.

With tears held back, I squeeze my dad's hand tighter, desperately wishing I could take away his pain and make everything okay. He never complains, but the agony he endures is visibly etched on his face. I cling to the hope that chemotherapy will provide some relief and foolishly entertain the idea that it will instantly shrink the abundance of cancer in his stomach. It's a feeble hope that I grasp onto, desperately searching for any semblance of optimism.

Reality sets in as the nurse calls out, "Mr. Kim? This way, please." It's his turn for observation and treatment. Holding his hand, my mom and I accompany him into the room. He climbs onto the examination table, where the nurse draws his blood and weighs him. As he removes his blazer and steps on the scale, it reads 165 lbs.—good enough. The nurse expresses satisfaction with his weight, noting that he hasn't lost too much.

We proceed to the observation room, where Dr. Midnight examines his stomach and reviews his charts. Never did we anticipate that a distended stomach would be a sign of cancer. She presses his abdomen, assuring us that it's stable for now, and promises to discuss the blood test results during the next visit. She reveals that his "tumor count" stands at 9—an obscure numeric value derived from the blood test, where lower numbers indicate better outcomes. The doctor informs him that he will need to come in for chemotherapy treatment every two weeks, alternating with check-up appointments every other week.

Dr. Midnight's presence brings a sense of comfort, as she makes us feel like she's actively on this journey with us, rooting for my dad's victory. She directs us to the other side of the building, where he will receive his first round of chemotherapy treatment. Along with this, she provides several prescriptions that we must pick up at the hospital promptly, adding to the six he already takes.

We move forward, armed with hope, medical papers, and a determination to fight alongside my dad every step of the way.

With a reassuring smile on his face, my dad turns to me and my mom, his voice filled with determination. "Don't worry, I will beat this. I'm not in any pain. Don't cry for me. No matter how hard it gets, I'll be okay. I promise."

I embrace him tightly and reply, "I know, I love you, Dad. Fighting!" Every day, I make sure to express my happiness and gratitude for having him as my dad. Leaving him behind is an agonizing task, as I fear that each glance back might be the last. I deliberately avoid looking at him, not wanting him to see how close I am to tears.

As my dad takes his designated seat to begin his treatment, the nurse prepares the IV, bringing out several needles and tape. She returns with a small, clear bag containing the chemotherapy that will slowly drip into his bloodstream. She is quick and efficient with her supplies and puts the needle into my dad's arm as if she's done it hundreds of times before. As the machine beeps to signal the start of the treatment, indicating it's working, I sit next to him on the nurse's stool and ask if it hurts. He assures me it doesn't and that he doesn't feel anything unusual. A few hours later, he says he is feeling sleepy and wants to take a small nap. I leave to join my mom in the waiting room, waiting for his call. The grueling six-hour process feels interminable, yet he continues to remain positive and ensures everyone else is ok. I bring in small snacks that my mom packed from home for him to nibble on during the wait.

Across from him is another patient receiving chemotherapy treatment. As the nurse is setting up his station, the chemo bag bursts open. The clear chemical splatters on the chair and onto the floor. The pumps designed to help move fluids through tubes are still attached to their bags as the chemical comes gushing out from what was supposed to be a contained area. Suddenly as if out of a movie, it's as if some poison had been released as everyone moves fast but quite calmly. The nurses have an emergency plan in place that calls for them to put on their hazard gear. A respiratory mask descends over her face as she puts on goggles, gloves, and a suit complete with boots. They wiped up the spill, and luckily the patient was not in the chair the minute it spilled, but he is already getting set back up for his treatment. It is baffling to think that for a nurse to clean up the chemo that fell on the floor would require them to get fully geared up, yet this chemical was being injected into cancer patients.

Once the chemotherapy treatment concludes, he slowly rises, and we make our way home. Success—we have overcome the first round of chemotherapy.

Never once does my dad utter the words, "Why me?" or express a desire to give up. It's more of a reverse reaction, with me constantly questioning, "Why him?" The moment we return home from the hospital, he settles into his chair, opens his Bible, and prays. This time, he falls asleep as soon as he reclines on the chair. Even in his slumber, he seems to be in pain. It breaks my heart. The doctor and nurse had informed us that side effects vary for each individual, but we must remain vigilant, keeping an eye out for anything severe or concerning.

CHAPTER NINE
Embracing The Unknown

The side effects that are expected to accompany the chemotherapy are far more overwhelming than we could have ever imagined. The thorough explanation we receive beforehand does little to prepare us for the reality of it all. The tiny print of the labels on the medicine bottles, usually ignored by most patients and their families, suddenly becomes extremely important. They provide a thorough explanation of what will happen when drugs are taken. A detailed description of what one might expect in terms of reactions to the medicines should be emphasized in big bold letters on the front of every bottle. The fine print is now our lifeline, as we race against time and medical complications.

Within just 48 hours of starting chemotherapy, we are all shocked to discover how debilitating the side effects are. His temperature soars from 102°F up to 104°F, leaving him feverish and drained of energy. He sleeps for extended periods, only waking when we purposely wake him to ensure he eats something before taking his medication. Before giving him all the pills, I read through the tiny list of potential complications for each: severe nausea, vomiting, headaches, memory loss, weakness in the limbs, increased sensitivity to light and sound, skin rashes, hair loss. But those are just the start of it. It feels as though each "possible" side effect is manifesting as an actual effect. Fevers become a daily occurrence, and his energy levels plummet, resulting in him spending most of the day in a state of sleepiness and exhaustion.

My dad has served as the pastor of New Light Baptist Church for 23 years, and his dedication to the church is unwavering. Throughout his entire tenure, he has never missed a church service or an early morning prayer. His entire life is devoted to the church, and he is willing to make any sacrifice for his beliefs. Even after being diagnosed with stomach cancer, he can't bear the thought of giving up. While early morning prayers are canceled due to his health, he insists on continuing with Sunday services without question. He stays up late, studying and preparing for each service, despite the challenges posed by his medications. I can't bring myself to ask him to take a break, hoping that if attending church gives him the will to fight, then it's worth it. Deep down, I know that the extent of his commitment to church will serve as a gauge of how much longer he has left to live. It's something he will never give up.

On the second Sunday morning in September, he dresses in his Sunday suit and tie, and my mom drives him to church as driving is now impossible. How many more Sundays will he have? Exhausted from chemotherapy, he conceals his pain and discomfort, delivering his sermon with the same passion as every previous Sunday. He doesn't want pity or sympathy, nor does he want the attention to be on his health. He asks us not to tell anyone about his disease, explaining that he will inform the congregation when the time is right. I struggle to comprehend how he could keep something so serious hidden. The word "cancer" sends chills down my spine, and if I could have enlisted the prayers of every person, I would have gladly shared the truth with everyone. But it's not my decision to make, and I agree to honor his request.

After service, he opens the doors of the church, greeting every person who attends and inviting them to stay for lunch. The doctor has advised that carbohydrates would be beneficial for him to maintain his weight, so I make a quick delivery run to Jason's Deli to get him his favorite baked potato. The regret washes over me, realizing that I should have done this for him earlier before he became so sick. I apologize in my heart, feeling a profound sense of sorrow. How many more opportunities will I have to share meals with him? It feels like a countdown, each meal becoming more precious as we face an uncertain future.

Yes! He successfully makes it through Sunday service, but the toll it takes on him is evident as he immediately collapses from exhaustion upon arriving home. My heart aches for him, yet I'm relieved that he can still engage in what he loves doing. I yearn to ask him to stop, assuring him that it's okay to take a break, but deep down, I sense that it would mean taking away something he truly wants. Let me just bite my tongue on this one and let him be. Whatever he chooses doesn't matter to me as long as he is alive. What more could I ask for? It seems just a matter of time before he will not have the energy for Sundays.

Every passing day becomes a testament to his unwavering fight for life, and I recognize that each day I have with him is a precious blessing. Yet, as time progresses, I find myself grappling with selfish thoughts, wishing for just one more day by his side. If the first round of treatment caused any discomfort, he kept it hidden from us. He wakes up each morning, fervently praying for everyone, and ends the day with a prayer of gratitude for the blessings bestowed upon him. I'm left speechless, witnessing how he can still find happiness and maintain unwavering faith despite his life being turned upside down by a disease that inflicts immense pain.

With one cycle of chemotherapy completed, we have nine more to go. The journey ahead feels daunting, but we remain steadfast in our determination to overcome each obstacle together.

My dad's perspective on life remains steadfast, and he never lets on to the extent of his pain. Not a single day passes without him letting me know, "I'm still here! I'll beat this, and I love you!" But no matter how strong he appears, it feels like a never-ending storm of anxiety, with each minute ticking by like a time bomb ready to go off at any second. My heart races faster as each day passes, knowing the future remains completely unpredictable. Nothing seems certain in my world anymore; I feel constantly on edge, struggling to brace myself for whatever outcome fate has in store.

The chemotherapy treatment completely weakened his body, and it enhanced the side effects of the medications. The drug-induced lethargy forces him to retire to bed earlier than he would have liked. His hair thins, his stomach lacks hunger pains, and waves of nausea follow him around like a cloud. The only inkling of comfort I find is when I return to the house from work, back to the house to see my dad patiently waiting for me. In those moments, I can finally catch my breath. He expresses concern for my well-being and inquires about what I had done during the day and if I had eaten anything. I would lie through my teeth, assuring him that I had eaten lunch every day, even though my diet consists of mere coffee and a Snickers bar, simply to silence the growling of my empty stomach. Hunger pains become inconsequential in the face of my dad's battle.

The passing of each day becomes a mystery as I witness the physical toll the treatments take on my dad's body. Yet, his concern remains focused on the well-being of his congregation and the happenings at church. He understands that the forthcoming chemotherapy sessions will grow more challenging, with the side effects intensifying sooner rather than later. Despite this knowledge, he dedicates Saturday nights to translating his sermons into English for those who don't speak Korean. The light from his desk lamp illuminates the room well past midnight as he immerses himself in the Bible, preparing for Sunday service.

There is a bittersweet realization that these moments of witnessing my dad diligently preparing for service may be limited. As much as I wish for him to rest, it is not within my right to ask such a sacrifice of him. This level of devotion is beyond my comprehension, yet if it keeps him alive and gives him purpose, I will not intervene. Though this image of him engrossed in his studies has anchored me since childhood, the battle takes its toll on my dad each day, as does the sorrow that engulfs me each day. Still, I am reminded that I can find happiness as long as he is still here with me.

The day arrives, ready to bring us back to the Cancer Center; however, this time we are not only coming for my dad's first chemotherapy treatment. We have also come to receive lab results from a sample of his blood as well as more blood for further analysis of its impact on the cancer cells. Nervousness permeates the air, but my dad remains composed and never shows any sign of anxiety or fear. He takes short walks up and down the hallway to keep his leg muscles from stiffening. My restlessness is on edge, threatening to overwhelm me. I want to leap out of my skin with impatience while counting down the minutes until we get our results. It was as if this would be our guide to how future treatments would be.

Several cancer patients are scattered about the room, some gripping their stomachs or supporting one another in a wheelchair while others hobble around the building with a cane. The air is wilted with despair and hope, yet my dad wears an expression that remains unwavering in his faith. Opening up to these strangers, he engages in conversations with cancer patients, offering words of encouragement and reminding them that God has plans for everyone, urging them not to lose hope. I sit back, observing with a smile the incredible person I have been blessed to call my dad.

A nurse appears from behind the door, calling for my dad to proceed to the examination room. Stepping onto the scale, it reveals a weight loss of five pounds in just one week, now at 155 lbs. It's not a drastic change, but maintaining his weight becomes crucial. Dr. Midnight enters the room, holding a clipboard adorned with a list of numbers that seem foreign to us. All we long to hear is that everything is alright and that he can go home without worry of further decline. The doctor explains that the side effects of chemotherapy are expected to intensify with each round, and I can only hold onto hope that my dad will weather the storm.

The doctor's words about the intensifying effects of chemotherapy seem to ring true as my dad's body begins to succumb to its weight. His energy levels deplete rapidly, leaving him confined to his chair or bed, where he falls asleep most of the day. Despite his efforts to conceal his pain, it becomes increasingly evident when he trembles and clutches his stomach, doubling over in agony. The prescribed medications, including morphine and Fentanyl, provide little to no relief, and I find myself suggesting a return to the hospital for further intervention. Fevers become a regular occurrence, as expected, but what catches us completely off guard is the onset of vomiting.

This is not the typical kind of vomiting we are accustomed to; it is the expulsion of black liquid, a disconcerting sight that strikes absolute fear. Contacting the hospital for guidance, we learn that this is a reaction of his body to chemotherapy and the acid in his stomach. The nurse advises us to monitor his condition and, if it worsens, to bring him back to the hospital. It is an agonizing dilemma, torn between the desire for the professional care available at the hospital and the comfort of being in the familiar surroundings of home. The thought of him being in the hospital brings a certain degree of relief, knowing that there would be a medical team readily available. However, the solace of being at home is something we all crave in these difficult times.

Status: Condition – Worse

The suffering intensified to the point where he experienced bouts of vomiting at any given moment. We had to keep a trash can nearby, lined with bags and newspapers, to catch the black liquid he expelled. His inability to eat was juxtaposed with the persistent vomiting, an unsettling contradiction. No measure we took could alleviate his pain or halt the relentless vomiting. All the medication caused him to have extreme blistering in his mouth. As if things were not bad enough, he had to take Nystatin, which was some sort of liquid medicine that was to treat infections of the mouth. He would have to take a dose and swish the medicine and retain the dose as long as possible to hope that it will help treat the infections. Hoping that this would alleviate some of the pain, it would follow with Lidocaine that would numb his mouth and throat. Minutes later, it was all in vain as he threw everything right up.

In desperation, I called his doctor once again, describing the escalating situation. Her response was clear: we need to take him back to the Cancer Center for immediate medical attention.

CHAPTER TEN
One Step Forward, a Million Steps Back

This unbearable existence, trapped in a cycle of fear and dread, is one I am desperate to escape. Every day brings more terror, and each night brings a new nightmare that paralyzes me in my sleep. I crave a single moment of peace to be able to take a breath without the crushing weight of worry pressing down on me. Every breath felt both precious and terrifying, leaving me wondering if this was how my dad felt, too.

Upon returning to the Cancer Center, the doctor gently pressed her hands against my dad's distended stomach, revealing the necessity of a feeding tube. This procedure would aid in maintaining his weight and ensure he received the necessary nutrients, given his diminishing appetite. She instructed us to acquire cans of Ensure, which would be administered through the feeding tube that he would have to get done at the hospital. The process sounded simple enough but even that came with its challenges.

The incessant bouts of vomiting the black liquid, his fading memory, and the constant need for sleep made finding his comfort at home an arduous task. It felt as though nothing we did provided him with relief, and the pain persisted unabated. Morphine patches aka Roxanol, Fentanyl, and the list of all the other medications did not lessen his pain at all. Marinol capsules that were to treat his nausea and vomiting were of no use.

The room is cloaked in a blanket of dread as the doctor reads through the harrowing reports. My heart sinks further and further into my stomach as he announces the devastating news: the numbers from his latest tests reveal a drastic increase in his white blood cell count, and his tumor count has skyrocketed from 9 to 21 in just one week. How can this be when we so diligently follow each instruction? The blow to my stomach is palpable, but I hold back the tears and summon all the courage I can muster to refrain from breaking down. We must return to the hospital immediately; there are no more treatment options to try here. The pungent vapors of vomit, sweat, and fever fill the air around us as he struggles to stay conscious against the relentless onslaught of illness. His body is failing at an alarming rate. We have no other choice- back to the hospital it is.

The trips back to the hospital seem endless – the Cancer Center and the hospital are becoming the norm. Pulling into the familiar hospital parking garage, a wave of uncertainty washes over me. How much longer will we have to endure this relentless journey? Every minute of the day feels like a prayer, a plea for my dad to defy the odds and become a miracle—a survivor among the few who triumph over stage IV stomach cancer.

My heart plummets as my dad steps out of the car and an immediate realization of what is about to happen hits me. The world feels like it has stopped around me in that moment as I watch him start to fall, unable to catch himself on the passenger side door handle. An agonizing thud echoes through my soul as he hits the ground and time seems to stand still. My head swims with terror as I scramble to his side, my entire being screaming for me to make it all okay. He looks confused and fragile, barely managing to stand with my support, and revulsion surges through me as I hate the car that has caused such a tragedy.

I feel as if this is a forewarning as to what is to come. The incident shakes us both to the core, a stark reminder of his fragile state and the fragility of life itself. We cling to each other, seeking solace and support amidst the uncertainty that surrounds us. It is in moments like these that the weight of our journey becomes all too real, and the strength to carry on becomes a heavy burden to bear.

On September 11th, we arrived at the hospital's registration desk, knowing that he would be admitted once again for the procedure. Ascending to the 7th floor, my dad greets the nurses and fellow patients with his characteristic warmth. In the room designated for his stay, he changes into the sterile hospital gown, readying himself for the impending surgery to insert the "j-tube" aka feeding tube. The doctors gather around his bedside, explaining the procedure to us in detail. Just as he settles, a nurse enters and informs us that he needs to be transported to a different level for the operation. Holding each other's hands, we follow behind as he is wheeled in a wheelchair, a stark reminder that nothing will come easily, and hope is all we have to cling to.

Upon reaching the designated area, he is transferred to a bed, and another individual enters the room, requesting his signature on a consent form. In the same breath, they mention the slim chance that he might not wake up from the surgery. It feels as though he is being asked to sign away with his life. The weight of the situation bears down upon us, and the fear in our hearts grows heavier. We nervously wait outside the surgery room, hoping and praying for a smooth and trouble-free process. Each passing minute feels like an eternity, and every time the automatic doors swing open, my heart skips a beat. The anticipation is overwhelming.

As my mother and I anxiously pace back and forth in the hallway, we cross paths with the first-year intern. He glances at us with a mix of sympathy and regret, apologizing for the circumstances. Summoning my courage, I muster the strength to ask the question that has been torturing me, though I fear the answer: "How much time does my dad have to live?"

The answer that I so desperately do not want to hear rips through the air like a dagger - "Probably a year. I'm sorry." My heart sinks into my stomach as we watch him walk away.

"No, no, no, this can't be true," echoes in my mind. I can't even imagine this world without him. A dark shadow of loneliness just spreads over me. I wish so desperately to turn back time. Only if I could remain in the shadows with him but I can't reach him. Every step is such a difficult step that is taking me away from him. The minutes in the day feel so long. All the things I'm used to only hurt me.

At that moment, an overwhelming sense of grief consumes me as reality settles - my father is dying. My heart aches with sorrow and regret for all the lost years and wasted moments. All the things I'm used to hurt so much.

Just one year? How can such a brief period be enough? My heart can't take the news, and I wrap my arms around my mom, tears flowing down my face, trying to bring her comfort as much as she's trying to bring me comfort. In our anguish, we know we have to be strong and wear happy faces in front of my dad, shielding him from the harsh reality we have just learned. The fear of how he would take this devastating news grips me, leaving me paralyzed in uncertainty.

As we wait for the doctor to come out and update us on the surgery, time seems to grind to a halt. The stillness gives us a moment to let our tears dry, but it offers no solace for the swirling emotions within. The suspense is unbearable.

Finally, after what feels like an eternity, the doctor emerges two hours later, delivering the reassuring news that the feeding tube has been inserted correctly. We are allowed to go in and see him. As we pass through the automatic sensor doors, I can't help but notice the other patients lying in beds, separated only by thin curtains, each grappling with their private struggles.

He is slowly waking from the anesthesia, and as soon as he sees us, a smile graces his face, accompanied by a small prayer of gratitude. Tears of relief well up in my eyes as I turn away from his bedside, trying hard to maintain a smile but failing as tears continue to fall uncontrollably. I feel like I am hanging on by a thread, my emotions teetering on the edge, while my dad faces countless needles in an absolute nightmare.

The world around me seems cold and dark, but amid this desolation, the warmth I find is in his sad and tired eyes. His strength and courage, even in the face of struggles beyond comprehension, become my guiding light. Despite the pain, he is there for us, comforting us with the fight to stay alive. When I touch his hand, it's so cold. I can't erase any of the hurt, all I can do is stay right by his side.

In those tear-filled moments, I realized that our bond transcends any darkness that life could throw at us. His love is an anchor, grounding me amidst the storms of uncertainty. I know that even when everything feels bleak, I have him by my side, and together, we will navigate the challenging road ahead. I know he understands my sad heart, as he tries to encourage me warmly with his eyes. Can he see my heart?

With each passing day it all seems to just pass by in a blur, my heart is both heavy with fear and uplifted by the love we share. Pain and sadness are constant companions, but so is the unwavering support we draw from one another. In the face of adversity, I cling to the memories of happier times, cherishing the moments of joy we have experienced together.

So, as we face this daunting journey, I vow to be a pillar of strength for him as much as he is for me. Heartbreak. Please stay alive. Every day I feel like I'm holding back my pain. Every day, I suppress my anguish and watch helplessly as he withers in agony. I can see the pain etched on his face, the exhaustion in every breath he takes. I try to hide my own anguish, but it is always there, lurking just beneath the surface. His eyes betray him - I can see the weariness etched deep within them - but he refuses to let it show. He doesn't want to make me sad. It's okay, I reassure myself, things can't possibly get any worse... until they do. In one moment, everything changes. He looks at me with confusion, barely whispering the words "Who are you?"

My heart stutters to a stop; I am not prepared for this. How could he not recognize me? The shock feels like a physical blow - a part of me dies right then and there. This isn't supposed to happen. He is supposed to know me. Nevertheless, I manage to keep my composure and reply calmly as if nothing happened.

"Hi daddy! It's me! Your favorite daughter is here!" I call out in a broken voice.

"I will be here every day no matter how hard it is. I hope you know I'll hold your hand the way you always have with mine." I whisper to him, "Every day I will wait for you."

My heart stops. That familiar face, which I have memorized each little wrinkle on, stares back at me questioningly. I did not think it to be possible for him to not remember me, but there he lay before me without the slightest recognition. My chest aches with loss but still, I smile at him and tell him as if nothing happened. "Hi Daddy! It's me! Your favorite daughter is here!" I manage to let out, grasping for the remainder of my hope and hiding my despair. A stranger looking into my eyes would see something different than how I am feeling but right then I need to maintain the cheerful attitude that always defines me even when everything else around me is falling apart. He keeps getting farther away from me. No. Don't go. I am not ready for my heart to ache so much just looking at him.

As if on cue, his eyes seem to stare back at me with recognition as he gives me a big smile. I ask him if he knows who I am, he whispers "Of course!" I miss his voice. It is now barely a whisper and so shaky. This is a step I'm not ready to take. I'm scared of closing my eyes and falling asleep.

The realization hits me like a battering ram, shattering my heart into a million jagged pieces. The days spent walking side by side with him, sharing stories, tears, and laughter are over - an unchangeable fact that delivers a crushing blow to my already fractured soul. I begin to realize how precious all those moments have been and bitterly wish I could go back in time to relive them, never wanting it all to end.

Despite what seems inevitable now, I hold tight to the hope that he will somehow make it through as he promised. Even though the future may be unclear right now, I keep fixed on the thought that tomorrow will bring new hope. I don't want to see the look of exhaustion in his eyes. I just want him to be with me every day.

CHAPTER ELEVEN
Weight of Silence

The process of filling the feeding tube with Ensure and then adding water to achieve fluid consistency poses its own set of challenges. We are torn between not wanting to dilute the supplement too much and risking inadequate nutrition versus the constant fear of clogging the tube and depriving him of vital nutrients altogether. As a result, his food intake plummets to absolutely nothing, and he becomes entirely reliant on water and the feeding tube. Witnessing this struggle is nothing short of a nightmare.

Unfortunately, despite our efforts, we soon discovered that the thickness of the Ensure nutritional supplement presents a significant challenge. It frequently causes blockages in the feeding tube, which requires us to flush it out regularly. The complications become so severe at times that he has no choice but to return to the hospital for a complete replacement of the tube. It seems that nothing comes easily in our quest to provide him with proper nutrition. The financial burden adds to the emotional turmoil we are already experiencing. The monthly rental cost of the feeding tube alone is $150, and that doesn't even include the cans of Ensure we need to constantly drip into the bag. The mounting expenses only add to our stress and worries during an already challenging time. Everything seems to be piling up at once. The cost of one shot that he has to have is already over $1,000! It is not even an option to not get the shot.

To make matters worse, he constantly encourages us to eat while he sits in his chair, his only company being a nearby trash can and the feeding tube bag that resembles the IV stands at the hospital, minus the wheels. It is a painful reminder of his current state and the stark contrast between our ability to consume food effortlessly and his inability to do so. There is no way in which any of us would eat a meal in front of him when he would not even be able to - that just seems to take it to another level of torture for him. We would all lie and tell him that we had already eaten.

As if to make the situation worse, the fevers keep on occurring daily. It is as if he has the flu and is sleeping most of the day. His hair begins to fall out, and the medicine makes him forgetful. Walking around the house is a chore, and all he wants to do is sleep. The few moments he is awake, it is as if he is trying so hard to appear normal, but the pain is too obvious. It feels as if we are all holding our breath in hopes that the pain will ease, but that is nothing but a faint dream.

The world seems to move in slow motion as we continue to stand by his side, our emotions torn between the agony of watching him suffer and the determination to provide him with as much love and comfort as possible. Hospital visits become a constant backdrop to our lives, and we navigate the complexities of medical jargon and treatment options, seeking any glimmer of hope that could offer a chance at a brighter outcome.

Mom goes ahead and shaves his head, and he makes it to the third round of chemotherapy. After the third round, the doctor tells us that it is too much for him, and he will need to rest for a month. It seems that the situation has improved slightly. We have gotten to the point where we are pretty much able to clean the area of the feeding tube and master the Ensure-to-water ratio without having it get clogged so often. The open wound around where the feeding tube is on his distended stomach seems so painful, but it does not compare to the pain from the cancer itself.

His diet, which had previously consisted of only bland foods - apparently salt is harmful to his body, so just taking out seasoning was nothing compared to now resorting to baby foods. He cannot hold it down, but he still tries, I think more to make us feel better as he throws it up a few minutes later. It seems such a struggle for him to do anything; even sleeping is too painful for him. The pain at times is so unbearable for him that it is as if he forgets where he is or what year it is. It is a total mess, even with him here I miss him. Every time I hear him whisper, I want to cry. The nights come with such anxiety that when he says he is going to sleep, I am on edge, wondering if this is going to be the last time.

My heart skips a beat as I enter the room. His still figure lies in the bed, not stirring at all - no movement. Fear and dread course through my veins as I call out to him with trembling lips but there is nothing. No response, not even a sound. I reach out slowly and place my hand on his chest, hoping against hope that he is still alive. The faint warmth sends a spark of relief through me, and I can feel a shallow current of breath move against my skin. …he does not wake up… I keep calling out to him, but he remains unresponsive.

My hands tremble as I grab the phone and punch 9-1-1 with an urgency that swallows me up. Tears well up in my eyes as the monotone voice at the other end says: "Please state your emergency."

I can barely choke out the words as they tumble from my lips. "My dad is not responding to anything! He won't wake up! I think he's dying! Please send help!"

The dispatcher asks questions about his hospice care and cancer diagnosis while dispatching an ambulance. She reassures me that help is on the way.

This is our painful reality, a never-ending wave of hope and heartbreak. We cling to the smallest glimmer of progress, cherishing any moment of relief. Despite our desires for a turnaround, we know that the struggle to survive is intensifying with each passing hour.

I sigh softly, wishing he would laugh and smile again. But as long as he is here with me, this will have to do. The more I try to hide my own emotions, the more it feels as if they are seeping out of me. I want so much for things to work out, but I know that this is completely out of my hands, and no matter what I do, the pain is still there.

Back to the Emergency Room we arrive, and immediately he is rushed through two doors that lead us straight to the Intensive Care Unit. It is a whirlwind of chaos and uncertainty, as two patients are assigned to one nurse. Soon, two doctors and a nurse came to the room, presenting us with a crucial decision to make right then and there – whether to proceed with a tracheotomy. They explained that they needed to put a tube into his lung to drain the fluids and that the situation is critical, as well as his need to have a tracheotomy.

They inform us that if he keeps the tube in his nose, it will lead to his stomach draining out the acid, but he will lose his ability to talk as it will rub against his vocal cords causing more pain and more medical jargon that is beyond comprehension. They say the tube that will go to his lungs would take out some of the liquid that is causing immense swelling. Once that procedure is done, he will be strapped to a hospital bed that will constantly invert him. This is too much to process. One explains that a tracheotomy is needed to allow him to breathe properly again and that this will allow him to talk. She tells us that we have made the right decision as there is no guarantee that the tube in his nose could be removed without doing serious damage. They reassured us that he would be able to speak after the procedure.

Without much time to process, we all agreed to the procedure. Little did we know that this would be the last time we would ever hear his voice again. The weight of the decision hangs heavily on our hearts, filled with hope that it will somehow improve his condition, but also knowing that it marks another loss – the loss of his voice, a cherished part of his identity.

The days that follow the tracheotomy are a whirlwind of pain and frustration for him. Instead of being able to communicate with words, he is faced with an insurmountable challenge - coughing and rasping that only brings forth a thick gloopy slime from his throat port. He has no choice but to rely on pen and paper for any form of communication, but his shaking hands due to the pain and medication make it impossible to write legibly. His attempt at writing resembles a jumble of tangled lines and indecipherable letters, each word feeling like an eternity as he tries to unravel them from the mess.

It is heart-wrenching to witness him grapple with this new way of expressing himself, as the frustration of not being able to communicate with his voice weighs heavily on him. We gather around him, trying to decipher the messages hidden within the chaotic scribbles, understanding that each word he writes holds immense significance.

After staying in the ICU for a week, there is a sign on the outside of my dad's door saying, "Put on gloves, gown, and mask before entering." It just seems so awful. How can I hold his hands with purple rubber gloves that keep me from touching his hands that always comforted me? As everyone puts on gloves and a gown, I put my gown on backward so that it ties in the front instead of the back, and I just grab two small purple gloves and a mask lying in the boxes just in front of his room. Rushing into the room, I cannot even force myself to put on the mask... how else would my dad see me smile? He presses the button to raise the bed into a sitting position and smiles, squeezing my hand.

A nurse walks into the room and sees me without the mask on. She tells me that I must put it on because my dad has MRSA (Methicillin-resistant Staphylococcus aureus) and that it is in the air, so we need to protect ourselves from getting it. She checks his IV stand and makes sure all the bags still have medicine in them and asks if he needs a shot of morphine. He nods his head, and she says that she will come back with the shot, reminding me to make sure I keep the mask and gloves on. No.

The air in the room feels heavy with precaution, and every interaction carries a sense of urgency and vigilance. Even with all the protective measures, I cannot help but feel the weight of fear and vulnerability in the room. I long to hold his hands without any barriers, to feel the warmth of his touch reassuring me that everything will be okay, but the gloves act as a tangible reminder of the invisible threat surrounding us.

As the nurse returns with the shot of morphine, I watch as my dad's expression softens, and he seems to find some relief from the pain that plagues him. It is heartbreaking to witness his suffering, but I am grateful for any respite he can find. At that moment, all I can think of is to take off the mask again and take a deep breath. The suffocating feeling of being hidden behind layers of protective gear overwhelms me, and I long to feel the air on my skin, unfiltered and unrestricted. Another nurse came in to prick his finger for some tests and then quickly left. The constant intrusion of medical procedures only added to the feeling of helplessness and desperation.

As the tears continue to well up in my eyes, I desperately try to turn away from my dad, willing myself to be strong and composed. The pain and sorrow seem to have a life of their own, defying my attempts to control them. My emotions are a turbulent storm inside me, and no matter how much I try to suppress them, the tears persist.

Taking a deep breath, I gather the strength to look at my dad again. I lean in and kiss his cheek gently, whispering the words "I love you" with all the love and support I can muster. His raspy voice, barely a whisper, reaches my ears as he speaks of how he is not experiencing much pain and expresses his unwavering determination to beat this disease. I place his hand on my cheek, wanting him to have some reassurance that we are in this fight together.

His hands, once so strong and capable, are now dry and worn, the nails still black from the medications he has been taking. I gently hold his hand in mine, massaging his swollen fingers, knowing that they must be sore from the countless needles and medical procedures.

The nurse pricks his finger to check his sugar level, but he barely winces, as if the physical pain has become a mere backdrop to the emotional turmoil he faces. I watch him endure it all with quiet courage, and it fills me with both admiration and heartache. Desperately, I rip off my gloves and scrape the metal side of the table until a sharp pain shoots through my finger. It is the least that I can do in exchange for the sea of emotion that crashes against his pale face. Hot tears run down my cheeks as I see a drop of blood on my finger, wishing that I could take some of this agony away from him. Knowing it is impossible and utterly foolish, the reality of the situation hits me hard - how can I even hope to lessen something he is going through if I am not even going through it with him?

He reaches for a piece of paper and scribbles with shaky, almost illegible handwriting, "I love you; I will beat this." Those words pierce my heart as I take it as a declaration of his will to win against insurmountable odds. I wish with all that upon everything, he will stay true to his vow even if it seems impossible. Now that he has lost his voice, I do not realize how much his words reach my heart. He used to always say that words can only survive if they reach one's heart and so to say things out loud. Those words I wanted to hear so much from him that everything would be ok – I will never be able to hear again.

CHAPTER TWELVE
Coming Home

As the doctor is explaining the arrangements with the home hospice, a sense of dread washes over me. The dreaded home hospice – I struggle to comprehend how the hospital insists on taking him home, relying on hospice nurses who will administer morphine pills when he's in pain. The prospect of bringing my dad home and caring for him with the limited resources of the hospice overwhelms me. They assure us the hospice nurses will provide morphine pills to manage his pain, but I can't shake the memory of how the pills took a while to take effect in the past. The more effective morphine shots he received at the hospital aren't allowed to be administered outside of that setting, adding to my concern.

My brother heads home to prepare for the hospice providers, who arrive to set up the equipment we need. Among the items are a hospital bed and a vacuum machine connected to the tube in my dad's nose leading to his stomach. Another vacuum machine, with a suction tube for him to hold, is provided in case he needs to expel anything. They also supply an oxygen tank for use when his oxygen levels drop. I quickly called another close friend,

Bekah, letting her know that my dad is finally coming home. She quickly tells me that she is on her way!

The hospice nurse explains the purpose of each piece of equipment, assuming we're unfamiliar with their use. However, after spending months in the hospital with my dad, we've become quite familiar with these devices. It seems the hospice has not taken the time to fully understand our situation, and their lack of attention to detail is concerning.

I have to call the hospice to request a second vacuum device, as they neglected to send it initially along with the device set to clean his trach band with steam. They seem dismissive of our needs and question why we require specific equipment. I insist on receiving a device to provide steam for cleaning his trach band, as it was used in the hospital to prevent mucus buildup, which could lead to pneumonia. Even when they finally send it, it doesn't provide the same pressure as the one from the hospital, leaving his trach clogged and causing mucus to overflow, requiring constant suctioning.

The sound of the approaching ambulance echoes through the walls of my house, and my heart races with anticipation. I rush outside, anxious to catch a glimpse of my dad as he returns home after months of hospitalization. As the attendants carefully lift him out of the back of the ambulance and roll him into the house on a stretcher, my dad's eyes scan the familiar surroundings, and a radiant smile spreads across his face. He mouths the words "my home" to the nurse and attendants, expressing his joy at being back in the place he cherishes.

Despite the difficult circumstances that led to his return home, I try to swallow the lump in my throat and brush away the tears that escape down my cheeks. His smile, filled with warmth and love, became the highlight of my life. I couldn't have asked for a more heartwarming welcome for my dad as he returned to the comfort and familiarity of his own home.

The ambulance drives away, leaving us standing in the doorway, a whirlwind of emotions inside me—gratitude, relief, and an underlying unease.

"He's finally home—even though he can't speak, at least he is home," I reflect, memories flooding back to when he wasn't sick, when every day was just a normal day, and he wasn't slipping away. The hospital bed is carefully moved into the living room, creating a makeshift sanctuary for my dad. The hospice nurse efficiently sets up the necessary equipment, including the IV to ensure he receives vital fluids. I wish I could turn back time.

But even with all the preparations, a heavy cloud of sadness and finality hangs in the air. As soon as the nurse finishes setting up, she hands me some paperwork, and my eyes immediately fixate on the bold letters: "DNR" – Do Not Resuscitate. The words seem jarring and harsh, a stark reminder of the reality we're facing. It feels wrong, and the weight of the decision seems unbearable.

The nurse kindly explains the implications, telling me that if something were to happen, they would respect our wishes and let him pass peacefully. The alternative is trying to revive him, which would likely cause him pain and discomfort.

The DNR form feels like an acknowledgment of defeat as if we're accepting the inevitable. It's a decision that we never wanted to make, but we have to come to terms with the reality of his condition. As much as we want to hold onto hope, we can't deny the truth.

In that heart-wrenching moment, I felt overwhelmed by a flood of emotions. The nurse's explanation feels like a cold, clinical detachment from the gravity of the situation. How can they expect me to make such a life-altering decision with my dad right there, so close, and yet so vulnerable? It's unbearable, and I feel completely overwhelmed.

My mom, standing beside me, is doing her best to hold back her tears. She, too, is struggling with the weight of the decision, but at least she has the composure to leave the paperwork for me to complete. However, I feel paralyzed by the enormity of the task before me. Every option on that form seems like an impossible choice, each one with consequences I can't bear to think about.

I want to scream, to run away from the room and hide from the pain and responsibility. The idea that one wrong decision could impact the rest of my dad's life is suffocating. There's no guidebook for this, no way to know what the right answer is. All I want is for the ground to swallow me up, taking me far away from this crushing reality.

But as I look at my dad lying there, fighting his battle with such strength and determination, a spark of defiance ignites within me. I can't let his life be reduced to a piece of paperwork, a mere checkbox on a form. No matter how overwhelming the situation, I have to stand my ground and advocate for what my heart tells me is right.

With tear-filled eyes, I turn to the nurse and gather the strength to inform her that we won't sign the DNR form. No matter what, we want them to do everything in their power to revive my dad if something were to happen. I know it might not be easy, and there could be regrets and doubts later, but in this moment, all we care about is the unwavering desire to keep him with us for as long as possible.

The nurse's expression of bewilderment isn't unexpected, but I can't let doubt or judgment sway my decision. This is my dad's life, and I'm determined to fight for it with every fiber of my being Looking back, I may wonder if I made the right choice, but at that time, it's a decision made from love, desperation, and a fierce determination to hold onto the precious time we have left with him. It's not an easy path, but it's the one we choose, and we'll face whatever consequences it brings with unwavering resolve. The future is uncertain, but in this moment, we choose to cling to hope and embrace the present, united in the strength of our love for my dad.

The living room that once held laughter, joy, and family gatherings now becomes a place of profound introspection and bittersweet moments. We cherish every minute we have with him, finding solace in the comfort of being surrounded by the familiar sights and sounds of home. We seek to make every moment count, expressing our love and gratitude through gentle touches, heartfelt words, and silent companionship. The familiarity of home cocoons his body as it succumbs to a disease even modern medicine can't defeat.

The atmosphere is laden with mixed emotions—sadness, acceptance, and a sense of togetherness as we confront the inevitable. We're determined to provide him with as much comfort and love as we can in these final days, even if our hearts are heavy with grief.

Amidst the DNR form and the acknowledgment of the reality of his condition, we cherish the precious time we have left with him. Every moment becomes a cherished memory, etched in our hearts forever. The journey ahead is difficult, but we're resolved to support him with all the love and tenderness we can muster, cherishing each day we have with him in the comforting embrace of home.

The weight of the situation bears down on me like an anchor, pulling at my heart with each passing moment. Despite my best efforts to stay strong, my composure feels like it's crumbling bit by bit. My dad's smile, though heartwarming, only magnifies the huge hole I feel tearing inside me. His presence alone has always been such a pillar of strength in my life, and now, with the looming uncertainty, it is now crumbling, leaving me exposed to an uncertain future.

As he lies in bed, he glances over in the direction of the piano and smiles. His finger, weak and shaking, slowly points towards it as if to tell me to play something for him. Playing his favorite songs for him becomes a bittersweet act of devotion. I'm terrified of playing. The fear that this may be the last time. I make an excuse and go to my room to hide for a minute.

Bekah comes into the room and hugs me, whispering, "Your dad has made it this far. He is fighting for you."

"I'm terrified of losing him. What if this is the last time?" I whispered to her, tears streaming down my face.

"Your dad needs to hear you play. You can do this. He loves you," she nodded in the direction of the living room where he was.

I move from one piece to another, wondering which would best express what is going on in my head: the fear, anger, or sheer sadness that has been threatening to tear me apart for the last 11 months. Every note that I play seems to land like a weight on my chest. I know that if he passes, I won't be able to bear the pain of playing the piano ever again. The notes resonate through the room, creating a haunting symphony that echoes the depths of my emotions. My heart feels so shattered that even tears seem unable to escape, leaving me feeling numb and lost. My fingers move effortlessly over each key as I try to drown out my thoughts with feelings of love and happiness instead of sorrow and regret.

Every song seems so bittersweet that tears keep falling from my eyes. Wiping them off my cheeks is useless; it never helps to stem the tide of emotions from pouring forth. After this, I know that the piano will turn into nothing but a memory of today.

My heart is gripped by desperation as I pray for a miracle, a way for my dad to escape the clutches of his illness and return to me in full health. Yet no matter how hard I hope, the truth of the situation remains still and silent. These moments I have left to spend with him will be forever scarred in my heart.

The brief moments of sunshine that marked his arrival home now seem distant and fleeting. Darkness engulfs us like an unwelcome guest, refusing to depart anytime soon. It feels as if a heavy cloud looms overhead, casting a shadow on even the simplest joys. As Bekah cautiously looks at me and asks if I need her to stay, my mind screams yes but I shake my head and tell her it is ok and that I would be ok. I didn't need her to see me fall apart again.

I've become a master at concealing my emotions from my dad, hiding my pain behind a mask of strength. But the façade becomes harder to maintain with each passing day. I fear that one day I will reach my breaking point, succumbing to the overwhelming weight of grief and sorrow. But I also know that right now is not the time.

CHAPTER THIRTEEN
Desperate Night of Unfolding Goodbyes

In the dimly lit room, the evening unfolds with an air of unease, and my dad's sleep is disrupted by a sudden surge in fever, sending us into a state of panic. Just hours after being discharged from the hospital with no further options for treatment, we face this terrifying situation. My mom rushes to get cold compresses to soothe his feverish body, but to our dismay, the air conditioning unit chooses this very moment to fail us. The room feels stifling, and the heat only adds to our sense of helplessness.

Murphy's law seems to be at its cruelest, piling on challenges when we are least equipped to handle them. It's 10 PM, and we can't find anyone to repair the AC immediately. I grab a fan to at least offer some relief while my mom scrambles to gather more ice packs. As I attempt to wake my dad from his feverish sleep, my heart sinks with each failed attempt. He remains unresponsive, and the realization hits me like a ton of bricks. This cannot be happening. Not now, not when I'm not ready to say goodbye. I don't even know how to say goodbye.

In that moment, all my attempts to keep a brave face for him crumble, and I allow my emotions to spill forth. Tears flow freely as I plead with him to open his eyes, to come back to us. But there's no response, and the silence in the room feels deafening. My grip on his hand tightens as if holding on could somehow keep him here with us.

Desperate to find help, I scrambled to locate the contact information the hospice nurse had given earlier. My hands tremble, and my mind races as I fumble with my phone to make the call. The phone rings, and I pray for someone to answer on the other end.

The weight of reality bears down on me, and I realize how fragile life truly is. We are at the mercy of circumstances beyond our control, and despite all our efforts, sometimes the outcome remains uncertain. In the face of this uncertainty, all I can do is hold onto hope, reaching out for any lifeline that might help us through this dark and trying moment. My dad's life hangs in the balance, and I can only hope that someone will answer the call and offer a glimmer of light in this darkest of hours.

"Hello?" She answers.

My voice cracked with grief as I responded, "My dad has a fever of 104 and it's not going down. He is unresponsive! What do we do?"

"This is the end; you will need to call 9-1-1 and go back to the ER as he may not make it," came the chillingly cold response that I was not prepared for.

Her words felt like a gunshot straight to my soul. I felt my heart drop into an abyss of despair that had been lurking around me for so long. How could this be the ending? It feels surreal, like a nightmarish movie unfolding before my eyes in real time. The hospice nurse's calm demeanor contrasts sharply with the storm of emotions raging within me. I try to steady my voice, but it trembles with fear and desperation.

"But... there must be something we can do, some way to help him," I manage to say, my voice breaking with each word. I can't believe that after everything, we are left feeling so helpless and powerless. I felt as if we were just taken back to the beginning.

A whirlwind of thoughts races through my mind. The hospital, with its clinical halls and fluorescent lights, has become a place of pain and suffering for my dad. It was the place where we received devastating news, and where we struggled with treatments and life-altering medical decisions. But now, it seems like our only option. I can't bear the thought of going back to that sterile, cold environment, where the answers may not be any different than before. I wish there was another way, a miracle that could save my dad from this agonizing fate. But reality sets in, and I know that we have to act quickly.

The realization hits me that I might lose my dad, my pillar of strength and the person who had always been there for me. The weight of the decision to call 9-1-1 and return to the ER is unbearable, but I know it's the only choice we have before we lose him at any given moment.

As I pick up the phone, my hands are trembling, and I feel as if I could not even dial 9-1-1 fast enough. The sense of urgency in my voice as I explain the situation to the dispatcher and let her know that every second counts. I'm desperately hoping that they would be able to teleport at this moment in time, but again my mind has practically lost all sense of practicality. I hang up the phone, tears stream down my face, and I feel the weight of the world on my shoulders. I know that there was a bigger chance that we would not get the outcome we had been hoping for, but I can't bear the thought of doing nothing and just watching him slip away.

While we wait for help to come, I hold my dad's hand tightly, trying to squeeze some life into them. Desperately hoping for even a slight finger movement. Nothing. I want him to know that he's not alone, that we are here, fighting for him with all our might. He looked so frail and as if he was just sleeping. Amidst all the crying, he doesn't even budge. This is so disheartening I don't even know how I am breathing. Every second that passes feels like an eternity, and I'm torn between desperately wanting them to arrive quickly and fearing that their arrival might be too late.

I hold my dad's hand, praying that he knows how much he means to me, and how much I love him. I hope that somehow, my love can reach him, even in his unconscious state. As the minutes tick by, my anxiety reaches its peak. I'm torn between the fear of losing him before the ambulance arrives and the desperate hope that the medical team will be able to somehow help him.

Finally, the sound of sirens pierces the night, and a glimmer of hope ignites within me. The paramedics arrive, and with a sense of urgency, they work to stabilize him before rushing him to the hospital once again. Time stands still as we wait for news on our drive to the ER once again, not knowing what lies ahead.

This nightmare is not going to end. A heavy weight is added to my heart, will he ever see this home again? He was so happy to have been brought home just days ago and only to leave unconscious. God help me, I'm breaking.

Everything seems hopeless but everything passes with time without noticing. I don't know what it is that I want but I hate myself and feel hopeless. The one person I would rely on to hold my hand and make me feel safe through all the hard times is no longer here for me and slowly disappearing before my eyes. I just want him to stay with me as my heart is already torn.

CHAPTER FOURTEEN
Beginning of the End

We return to the ER, and the nurses and doctors work to revive him. His temperature is under control, and he's back on the IV with medicine being pumped into his port. The visitation hours have become irrelevant, as the nurses are now accustomed to my unscheduled visits and sneaking in to see my dad at any given opportunity. I sit beside him, holding his hand as he sleeps, expressing my relief that he's fighting so hard to stay alive. I'm too scared to voice the thoughts going through my mind; guilt floods over me. Speaking them out loud feels like I'm manifesting them into reality, intensifying the fear of losing my dad.

The nurses inform me that a room had become available on the 7th floor and that they would be able to move him in a few hours.

Relief… this means he's out of the "critical" phase. Despite not lasting 24 hours at home, seeing him smile makes it worthwhile. At least he was able to come back to the house even for a day.

Back on the 7th floor, the familiar cancer ward, a wave of relief envelops me. My dad may have been through another harrowing episode, but at least he's alert and under supervised care. As I sit by his side, I hold his hand and softly reassure him of my happiness that he's made it this far. Seeing him smile a faint smile, even for a moment, means the world to me.

Guilt gnaws at my heart, a relentless predator. The mistakes of the past, unintentionally hurting him, haunt me. The weight of these actions fills me with remorse, especially now that the opportunity to apologize may have slipped through my fingers.

Life's brevity becomes painfully apparent. It's an unforgiving reminder of the preciousness of time, and the fact that we should cherish every moment with the ones we love. I wish I could turn back time and undo the pain I caused, but I know that it's not possible. All I can do now is to be there for my dad, offering him love, support, and as much comfort as I can.

The routine beeping of machines is familiar now and oddly calming. The chaos that once overwhelmed me has turned into a sad, mechanical melody, and I find myself resetting the IV and checking the TPN bag with ease. The machines are now easy to operate and the names of all the medicines are just second nature as I can remember which meds were needed simply by the look of the pill or bag. It's become a part of my life, this new reality of caregiving.

As I massage my dad's weak and thin legs, I can't help but notice the toll the disease has taken on his once-vibrant appearance. His face is swollen, the color drained, replaced by a pallid yellow hue. The metal hospital bed rattles from his shallow breaths, sounding like a death rattle. Cancer's relentless advance tears him apart, and there's nothing I can do to stop it. Machines beep around us, clinical staff move with efficiency in their practiced routine, each action emphasizing the inevitability of what is to come.

The pain in my heart is unbearable. I forced myself to remain strong for him, but I didn't know how much longer I could keep it all together. The lump in my throat felt as if had become a permanent fixture. I wanted to cry, to scream, to let it all out, but I couldn't show him my emotions because he was already going through so much. Instead, I wipe away my tears with his hand, the hand that used to hold mine, and make everything okay.

I miss the days when he would open his eyes and smile at me, reassuring me that everything would be fine. But now, he's too weak to respond, and I miss even the slightest squeeze of his hand, a small gesture of comfort that I once took for granted. Finding the right words eludes me. How do you tell someone you love that you're terrified of losing them? That you wish you could join them on this painful journey to the end? I swallow my emotions and try to sound strong, assuring him that everything will be okay and that I'm waiting for him to come home.

I hold back, trying to protect him, even though he can probably sense my feelings. I want to share my day with him, to tell him everything that's on my mind, but I'm afraid. My mind screams, "Don't die and leave me. I'm scared. Please just don't die." All I can manage to say is "Please listen to my wish and wake up, Daddy. Just like you promised you would." hoping against hope that he'll fight a little longer.

The room grows deathly silent as I beg, pleading for a response from him. My heart thumps loudly in my chest and a single tear escapes down my cheek until his eyes flicker open. His mouth curves into a faint smile and I cry out in relief. I clutch onto his hand, desperate for a sign that he's still here with me, and I feel the feeble touch of his fingers barely squeezing back - a symbol of strength that fills me with warmth despite its fragility. The moment holds more value than anything else in this world. When I hear his breath, I feel like I can breathe again.

The emotion I feel is too overwhelming to bear, and a fresh wave of tears falls when he mouths the words "I'm sleepy." I tell him it's ok and to go to sleep. Every ounce of strength in his frail body is harnessed to keep fighting against the illness. As I gaze upon his slumbering form lying helpless in the bed, all the years of my inexcusable wrongs come flooding back. Shattering sorrow begs for redemption. How will I ever make it through life without having him here? My heart feels broken into a million pieces and despair takes over every thought. How can life ever be the same without him?

But even with this glimmer of hope, I can't escape the overwhelming fear of losing him. I wish I could have made him proud, but I can only hope he knows how much I love him. The future feels daunting and uncertain. I feel broken, but I try to hold on to the strength I have left, to be there for him until the end.

Time for me to go home and with a smile plastered on my face even though my heart was tearing inside I let him know, as I always have the past 11 months.

"Bye Daddy! Stay strong and sleep well. I love you and I'll see you tomorrow!" His eyes light up as he gives me a weak smile and a nod. Oh my God, my heart hurts so much. Slowly, I get up and make my way out of his room, looking back at him and hoping that tomorrow will come soon enough. Will he be able to come home again?

I wish I could find some sense of hope, some glimmer of light in the darkness. But all I can do is hold on to the memories. I'm trying to keep myself together, but this sense of dread just feels so heavy. This was not getting any easier.

I run into my dad's room after leaving work early, my mom is sitting in the chair beside him reading the Bible to him while holding his hand. As I come near the door, I announce my arrival as I always have "Daddy! I'm here!" As always, he opens his eyes and even with no voice, he smiles a weak smile and I see the smile in his eyes as if he had been waiting for me all day. What more could I ask for than to have him smile at me? I can't even begin to think about how my days will be when he will not be there waiting for me.

I tell my mom to go home and get some rest as I would be there with him until I was told to leave. I start to sing to him and massage his hands and legs. His warm hands would always hold my forever cold hands and make me feel so safe. His fingernails had slowly grown back pink as if to let me think that he was getting better. The tiniest glimpse of hope is what I seem to live for. I put his hand on my cheek and rub my face against his hand so he can feel my face, and he looks at me and mouths "I love you" with sleepy eyes, I ask him if he wants to take a nap and he nods his head.

"Get some sleep, Daddy. I'll be right here," I whisper and continue to sing.

The night stretches on, seemingly frozen in time, and I find myself walking the halls, lost in my thoughts. I remember how he used to make me smile, just by being there, without needing to say a word. His presence was a source of warmth and comfort, but now, that warmth is fading, and the comfort I once felt is slipping away. I'm left to face this pain on my own, with no one to lean on. The days of walking together on the cancer floor with the IV pole in hand seemed like a dream.

I ran into a nurse on duty, and I asked her, "How long do you think he has? He's barely woken up at all today." I know I'm grasping for any amount of hope from anyone that can offer me. I completely regret having asked this question as her response hit me so hard that I could barely catch my breath. Her response: "I think it will be difficult for him to make it past a few more days."

I immediately call my mom and as I fight to hold back the tears. I let her know what the nurse had just told me and that he was sleeping. I told her she needed to hurry back to the hospital just in case what the nurse said was true.

As I walk back to his room, I wipe the tears off my face and call the church phone knowing that I will get to hear his voice. I wish I could turn back time to any moment before he lost his ability to speak just to hear his voice once more. I listen, and then I hang up. I call back again to hear it again and then hang up. God help me. I can't bear the thought of losing him.

The weight of my pain presses down on me like a million bricks, suffocating me until I feel like I can't breathe. I'm sure my heart will burst. I try to keep it all within, a silent struggle of wills that nobody else knows about. The pain is too great, the grief too deep - I have to do everything I can to keep myself together because if my dad sees how much this is hurting me, he'll be brokenhearted himself. Everyone around me is asking why I'm not showing it. They don't understand that the only way to protect the ones I love from pain is for me to keep mine locked away. People say that bottling up emotions only leads to disaster, but this time it's different. My pain is something I will eventually have to confront, though not at the cost of letting my dad see that I'm hurting too. He must think that his survival offers hope and strength to those he loves, even if it breaks me in the process.

Another nurse walks into the room and then looks at my dad and touches his feet which were ice cold. She then tells me "It seems like this is his time." I sat there shocked and unable to move. What was that supposed to mean? Who the hell was she to tell me this? What kind of person would tell me that? I did not want to comprehend any of this. As I walk out behind her I ask her what she is talking about, and she says that his legs will get colder and become colorless meaning less blood circulation. I look anxiously down the hall hoping to see my mother, but not yet. I hurry back to the room as I'm not ready to handle this alone.

"Daddy, I'm back!" I say as I lean to kiss his sunken cheek. My tears are falling against his cheek, but I can't stop the tears. Sigh. I cry "You promised to never leave me and that you would beat this. Who will I have to comfort me now? No one will understand how I am!" If loving someone hurts this much, I do not know how to deal with loss as broken as I have become. Will I ever be ok after this? He doesn't even move. His cheek is wet with my tears.

My mom bursts into the room as if she had wings on her back, tears falling like rivers down her face. She refuses to let go of his hand, and I call him again and again until he stirs from his sleep. When his eyes open, he sees my mother and brother standing by his side, and no matter how weak his body is, a smile peeks onto his lips.

We massage his legs and hands gently while I sing softly to him, repeating one thing over and over: that I love him. He looks at my mother who offers to stay with him until he sleeps for the night. He looked so peaceful and happy that we were all there. My mother whispers her promise that she will stay with him all night, and he mouths back that he is sleepy and wants to sleep.

"Good night, Daddy! I love you! Fighting! I'll see you tomorrow!" I whisper as I walk slowly away from the room. As the door closes behind me, it feels like a final curtain coming down: final.

CHAPTER FIFTEEN
The Last Smile

Everything is being torn apart; the pain knows no boundaries.

The shrill ringing of my phone pierces through the silence of the room, making me jump out of my skin. Adrenaline pumps through my veins as I fumble for my phone, trembling hands barely able to grip it. The call that will forever alter my life.

On the other end of the line is my mom's voice, trembling with fear and complete panic, "Your dad is not waking up," she gasps, her words permanently etched in my mind. "I can't get him to wake up! I keep begging him to wake up, but he's not moving. I need you to come to the hospital. Please, come quickly!"

A fear unlike any I've ever known before spreads through my veins, demanding that I get to the hospital as soon as possible. In a frantic plea to God, I ask that my dad wait for me - if I don't make it to the hospital in time, will he hold on until I do? Please wait. Daddy, please wait.

Who knew that yesterday would have been the last night for me to say any words to him? If only I could have stayed there all night and whispered in his ear all night how much I love him and thank him for being the best person I have ever met and the best dad a girl could ever have.

Will he wait? I'm drowning in so much pain; that I can barely breathe. As much as I've waited for a miracle, I know he is trying to leave me. This is one road I don't want to cross, as I know there is no way back.

I just freeze, unable to move. I just keep working away until I hear my friend Nola whisper, "You need to go. He's waiting for you." My body quivers in agony as I am terrified of what will happen if I go.

"If I go now, he will die. Maybe if I wait just a little longer, he will hold on and live a little bit longer waiting for me," I answer back. I clutch my chest as waves of despair crash over me. She puts her hand on my shoulder and tells me that it is time for me to go and to stop making my dad wait.

I pray for someone, anyone, to make the pain stop. But all I'm met with is a deafening silence that echoes through me like an icy chill. My mind begins to break under the crushing weight of this overwhelming pressure, and I fall onto the ground, utterly defeated. I feel her hug me as I crumble. I feel as if this is out of a movie where I know he is waiting for me, but my ultimate fear is that once he hears my voice – he will leave me. I'm not ready for this. I want one more tomorrow.

I launch myself out of work, tears streaming down my face, and ignoring the time. I stumbled through the parking lot in a desperate search for my car. Somehow, by sheer determination, I made it to the hospital and sprinted into the building. In a frenzied haze, I make my way to his floor, and as I have done every day before this, I start calling his name. I can feel my breath getting rapid and shallow as I pass by patients and visitors on my way towards him. My eyes travel over to the machines monitoring his oxygen level, his heart rate - the only source for any peace of mind that he is alive.

"Daddy! Your favorite daughter is here. I'm here, Daddy! Please don't leave me." My throat clamps around an impenetrable lump that rises from within me or maybe it never left.

As soon as I enter the room, he is just lying there as if he's asleep. My mom is on one side of the bed begging him to wake up and telling him that I am here. I can't stop crying with one hand holding his and the other touching his face and saying, "I'm here, Daddy. Please wake up. Don't go." His face is so tired and yet so calm as if he is in no pain. This feels so wrong.

All the other days his eyes would light up the minute I walked into the room, but today I don't get any response. I'm not ready … not yet…not now.

"No! No! No! No! Do you recognize me? Do you see me? Daddy!!! I'm so sorry for not coming sooner. You said you would fight for tomorrow. It's tomorrow. Today is tomorrow! Please wake up. I need one more tomorrow." I scream, and holding his hand, I use it to wipe my tears. I put my cheek on his cheek and have my tears roll down his face as I beg for him to wake up.

I lean over to put my arms around him and hug him as my tears are now soaking his hospital gown. I cry into his ears, "What do I do? Please recognize me. Open your eyes. I don't know what I'm going to do if you don't know who I am. Please wake up. You promised that you wouldn't leave me and that you would beat this. You said you would never let go of my hand. I'm waiting for you. Daddy...you promised."

Everything just feels so wrong. "I'm right here Daddy. I can see you. I know you are tired, but please wake up. Can you hear me? What am I going to do when I can't see you tomorrow?"

Silence. Not a single movement.

Time kept going but my heart just stopped. The nurses didn't come in to check on him, so something must be wrong….3:30 p.m.…A nurse finally walks in and goes to his IV pole that has several bags hanging and puts on another large bag filled with white liquid. I asked her what she was doing, and she said that this is the TPN that I requested. They bring a nutrition bag when they clearly can see that he is not responding. How is it that I had to ask that they get this to him and why did they not do this any sooner? Why could they not have given this to my dad months prior instead of the Ensure cans? What the hell is wrong with everyone? Or was it just me?

The doctor strides into the room and reaches out his hand for me, but I'm frozen in shock. He speaks to me, but I scarcely understand his words -- only that he will try something one last time to see if my father wakes up. He places a long suction tube with a camera at its end inside my father's lungs, as if trying to prove there is nothing left to do. With trembling hands, I wipe away tears so I can look through the tiny lens of the camera. All I can make out are faint shapes clouded by my relentless sobs. My mother holds him tight, her pleas muffled against his chest: "Wake up! Please wake up! Your daughter is here!"

Another doctor enters and approaches us. They both extend their hands in a gesture of sympathy, offering a silent apology before they turn around and leave the room.

The room seems to be spinning and nothing seems to make any sense. The machine showing his oxygen level and heart rate starts to ring in my ears -- just an obnoxious beeping sound that seems unceasing. The numbers are dropping in front of my eyes. I half climb into the bed with my dad and brush his face with my hands the way he would mine and kiss his cheek and whisper "Please wake up I'm here. Daddy. I need you. I need you! You can't leave me! You promised."

Nothing.

If only I could have traded places and God had taken me instead or at least let me have suffered it alongside him that way he wouldn't have ever been alone. Tears stream uncontrollably down my face; my nose runs with the flood of salty water. The very idea that I can still produce tears shocks me.

"Please wake up. I need you. Please wake up so I can tell you I love you again. Don't go. . . I love you." As I lay beside him in his hospital bed with my hand touching his sleeping face, I felt as if my life had just slipped away along with him. It couldn't be true, this was impossible. He was awake and responsive last night…there is no way he would leave me like this. Everyone told me that he was gone but I couldn't accept it, the doctors had to be able to do something! I could hear his heartbeat and his chest was moving. One of the doctors in the room went on to tell me that he would bring a video camera that he would put down his throat through the trach opening to show me that his heartbeat was slow and that it was time as he could not feel anything anymore and was gone.

Just like the wind, here for a moment and now gone. He is my everything.

The fog of grief that has been hovering around us for months thickens as we gather around him. His battle with cancer is finally over, but his loss leaves a hollow void in our hearts. My head feels like it is underwater, and the quiet stillness around me is broken by the sound of crying coming from my family. We all knew that this moment would eventually come, but it doesn't make it any easier. I had held onto hope for so long that he would beat the cancer and come home to us and yet here he is lying lifeless in this hospital bed.

I wish he had made it like he promised he would, and I'd get just one more look from him, telling me that everything was going to be alright. Every day felt like an eternity yet also so fleeting, from the diagnosis to now. 11 months had passed - the longest and the shortest time ever. With one last glance at my dad, I silently wished for something that could never be— just one more hug telling me everything was going to be alright. I want just one more something…a day…an hour…minute…just one more look from him telling me that I'm going to be ok.

At least the night before I had the chance to see his last smile, I told him as I left "Good night, Daddy! I love you! Fighting! I'll see you tomorrow!"

The only difference was that tomorrow never came. On this day, my time stopped – left with a painful wound that would never be cut or healed. I am just hurting, wandering, and crying as the sadness is like poison to my heart from missing him.

To you Daddy – I will always pray for you even though this painful wound that you left me will never heal. The words I couldn't tell you, the words I kept in my heart, and that I wanted to tell you – I miss you every day and I missed you even when you were here. I couldn't bear to tell you that I missed you when you were next to me, but I miss you. I so wish that you would have come back. The endless time I endured alone would have all been ok as long you would have been here.

The memories I have with you are nothing but a dream that goes away as soon as I wake up. The day you left me, I felt a huge part of my heart collapse. One day I was standing with you and walking the halls next to you and now I am left standing alone with nothing but the mere shadow of what used to be.

My heart aches and I can't think clearly. I want to see you, but you aren't here. Every day I'm just waiting for you. I'm standing by your empty space waiting.

I still remember the sad face I put on that day … is this how I will continue to feel? I feel as if the past will be forgotten … What I would give to just see you one more time. Spend one more day or even one hour just to hear your voice. How am I to go on and put the pieces of my heart back together again after it's been shattered?

Unreachable dreams are so heartbreaking – holding my breath with the false hope that my you would overcome cancer and make it out alive. The seasons are all going to return but without you, as I am left behind… this is how we part. It's so hard getting by each day. I'm so thankful for growing up as your daughter, please don't worry about me. I will take care of mom and do what I can to make her happy and keep her from being too sad from losing you.

Now I'm standing here by myself in the deep places of my memories. I want to go with you. I'm so tired and you left without a sound. No one is waiting for me now; I want to just go to you. Life is now incredibly exhausting, and I know that I'm at the end of this road alone. You are no longer here, and I can't even see you. The only reason the days would shine is because I knew I could go see you, but this sadness is so deepening. Fate did not spare me from being the sole straggler left behind on this road.

I hoped you could be here every day. In all my special moments I wanted you to be here as you were my everything. Even during the hardest times, you were always there. I won't ever forget. There's always another side to the story – I can only see what is visible to me – but there is a hidden beauty behind what we can't see which is the truth in life and the fact that you fought so hard to stay alive. You gave me countless gifts of "tomorrows."

Rest In Peace Daddy

Born in South Korea March 05, 1942 – August 4, 2007

SIXTEEN YEARS LATER

"Mommy, do you remember how you held in your tears with grandpa so he wouldn't know how you feel?" he asked.

"Yes."

"Well now we know where those tears went," he continued "your tumor."

Silence.

"Mommy, do you hurt?"

"Yes sweetie, a little."

"Mommy, I don't know if I want you to die or to live. I don't want you to die because I will be sad and I will miss you too much, but I also don't want you to live hurting so much all the time. Dying is the only way you will get some rest."

I think my heart just melted.

ABOUT THE AUTHOR

Fueled by an unhealthy amount of ice coffee, the author is a phantom lurking in the shadows of creativity, leaving traces of life behind in the form of words on these pages.

Life handed me a plot twist that rewrote my narrative—I had to rediscover the art of walking. Beneath the cloak of physical challenges, I found strength, not just in my steps but in the unknown.